LAB PARTNERS

LAB PARTNERS

M. MONTGOMERY

wattpad books W

Published in Canada by Wattpad Books, a division of Wattpad Corp.
36 Wellington Street E., Toronto, ON M5E 1C7

www.wattpad.com

First Wattpad Books edition: March 2020

ISBN 978-1-98936-514-4 (Softcover original)
ISBN 978-1-98936-515-1 (eBook edition)

Library and Archives Canada Cataloguing in Publication information
is available upon request.

Printed and bound in Canada

1 3 5 7 9 10 8 6 4 2

Cover design by Sayre Street Books
Cover illustration © Jason Flores-Holz
Typesetting by Sarah Salomon

For those who feel like they don't have a voice.

IDIOT GOLDMAN

"All right, everyone," Ms. Dailey announced from the front of the classroom. I had been scribbling absentmindedly in my notebook, which probably wasn't the best idea since this class was proving to be considerably more difficult than what I was used to. Up until now school had been easy for me, but this was my first college-level course, and for the first time in my life, I had to figure out what studying was. "We have now reached the end of the first marking period. You may remember that at the beginning of the year I promised to assign you new lab partners at this point." Some of my classmates started getting excited, hoping they might be paired with their friends, while others seemed less enthused by the possibility of being paired with someone they didn't like. In fact, the biggest reason Ms. Dailey was changing our lab partners was because of the people who were unhappy with their current lab partners. "Now, I don't want to hear any complaints. These changes will last until midterm."

I snuck a glance at my current lab partner, Walter Addens, and felt relief knowing that I wouldn't have to sit by him anymore. He was a nice guy and all, but his short black hair was always greasy and he smelled like he hadn't been near a shower a day in his life.

"The list of your new lab partners is posted on the door. Be sure to look at it before you leave today. Seating arrangements will be changed on Monday." As if on cue, the bell rang. "Have a good weekend, everybody."

Ms. Dailey walked calmly back to her desk as the room erupted into chaos. Everybody rushed to pack up their stuff and leave.

"See you later, man." Walter gave a small wave as he slung his backpack over his shoulder. "Oh, and here's your pencil back. Thanks for letting me borrow it."

"No problem, Walter. Have a good weekend."

"You too, Elliot."

I sat back in my chair and watched the tall, lanky boy fight his way to the door. Getting to the door wasn't that hard, as his odor made people naturally clear a path for him. He would've been fine if he just started using deodorant, but unfortunately, I don't think he got that memo in middle school.

The side of Walter's face was still visible to me as he read the list. I watched him as his eyes scanned the paper, thinking his facial expression might reveal something about his new partner, but he remained impassive, turning to leave once he had seen the name.

I waited for the next throng of sweaty teenagers to clear out before checking the list. Other people tended to make me feel uncomfortable, especially when they invaded my personal space. I closed my notebook and slid it into my backpack at a leisurely pace. Then I sat back in my seat and watched my classmates with mild curiosity.

They were all crowded around the door, trying to find out who their new partners would be. A couple of girls squealed excitedly when they learned they were paired with their friends, and a few guys groaned in frustration at the names they found listed beside their own.

Ms. Dailey was infamous at Pinecrest for pulling stuff like this: "creative" ways to "inspire" learning. Dreading the work was one thing, but forced partnerships and having to be part of a team was quite another. Still, as long my new partner smelled better than Walter, I would be all right—unless it were Morgan Cook or Nate Anderson. Both of those boys hated me. They made it their mission to make my life an absolute hell, along with another friend of theirs, Cole. Thankfully, though, he was not in AP Chemistry.

The minute hand of the clock hanging on the wall to my right ticked slowly; it was fitting—sitting in science class feeling the actual, physical pressure of time. I had approximately seven minutes until I missed the bus and would have to walk the four miles home. Begrudgingly, I pushed my chair back, grabbed my backpack, and walked to the front of the room.

There was now a little more breathing room by the door, since most of my classmates had seen the list and left already, but I still had to peer over a few heads to find my name. It didn't take long for me to spot it.

Elliot Goldman.

I flicked my eyes to the corresponding name and was relieved to find it was neither of my tormentors. A few years ago, I was partnered with Nate for a biology lab. I ended up doing most of the work and later found that he had snuck some frog guts into my backpack when I wasn't looking. I tried to get the smell out for weeks but ended up having to get a new backpack. I was glad I wouldn't have to worry about what he might do with chemicals for at least a few more months.

Jordan Hughes.

Interesting. Jordan had recently transferred here from out of state. If the gossip about him was anything to go by, he was from somewhere in the New England region. New Hampshire, maybe? I wasn't sure. I found it kind of odd, though, that he would be transferring into AP Chemistry after having missed out on the entire first marking period. Advanced Placement classes were no joke, and if most of us were struggling after having been here for two months, then he was surely doomed if he hadn't been taking it at his other school.

For his sake, I hope he had been, because I definitely wasn't in the mood to be pulling all the weight in our labs.

At my locker, it only took me a few seconds to spin my combination into the lock. I lifted up the latch, opened the locker, and was about to reach for my textbooks at the bottom when the door was suddenly slammed shut. Someone behind me laughed.

Immediately, I was face to face with Morgan Cook, who apparently thought slamming my locker shut for the hundredth time was the funniest thing he'd ever seen.

"What're you up to, freak?" he said. He folded his beefy, gym-jacked arms over his chest. He was a football player, and while some of the students on the team remained their scrawny teenage selves, that was definitely not the case for Morgan, who had nearly doubled in size since the start of middle school. His impressive physique was likely the reason he was assigned the position of defensive tackle. There weren't many others on the team who could hold the line as effectively as he could. But it wasn't hard to figure out that the brawn was making up for lack of a brain, especially when he opened his mouth.

"Oh, you know, just trying my best to avoid imbeciles like you," I said, turning back around and putting in my combination a second time. Once done, I tried to open the door again and was not at all surprised when he slammed it shut once more.

"You want to say that again, Idiot Goldman?" he growled.

"Was that supposed to be a clever insult?" I asked. "Because look, I can do it too. Morgan Cook? More like Moron Cook."

He didn't look happy.

"Actually, I think I read somewhere that guys with names that are more common for girls tend to be more aggressive and troublemaking than those with more masculine names. I personally think that explains a lot. Don't you?"

Morgan's fist strained at his side, and he was just about to cock it when the football coach walked by. Coach Hanover was an aging man with wispy salt and pepper hair. His eyes were recessed deep in his skull, and that, in combination with his low, bushy eyebrows and the wrinkles around his eyes, forehead, and mouth, made him appear all the more intimidating. As I wasn't in any sports, I hadn't interacted with him much, but he had been the gym teacher for my first year of middle school, and from what I'd seen of him, he was not someone to mess with.

"Cook!" His voice was like a bullet with how much power and intensity it held. It was so authoritative it could've quieted a whole pep assembly without needing to use a microphone. Morgan immediately straightened his spine and shifted his full attention to his football coach. Even I found myself standing a little straighter. "If you're not on the field by the time I get out there, I'll have you running laps. You know how I feel about tardiness."

"You've got nothing to worry about, Coach," Morgan said in a strong, sure-of-himself voice. Coach gave him a hard, warning glare before heading to his office. Once the older man rounded the corner, Morgan returned his glare to me. Just in case Coach Hanover was still in earshot, he lowered his voice so only I could hear him and grumbled, "We will continue this conversation later." Then he backed away and hurried off toward the locker room so he could get changed into his uniform before his coach made it back and decided to punish him for taking too long.

"Bye, Cookie." I waved, teasingly, my mouth distended in an exaggerated grin. Death wish or not, I couldn't help myself. Sarcasm was my only defense, and the mindless brute made comebacks way too easy. I spun my combination for the third time, this time successfully grabbing the textbooks I needed and shoving them into my backpack. Then I grabbed my hand-me-down dark-blue University of Michigan sweatshirt, tossed it over my head, and got the hell out of there.

I was just in time to watch the last bus pull out of the parking lot.

"Dammit," I said under my breath. The last thing I wanted to do was walk four miles home. I contemplated texting my sister to come pick me up, but then I remembered it was Friday, which meant she wouldn't be getting out of her classes at Kalamazoo Valley Community College until six. We were twins, but since she was smarter than me, she tested out of high school early and was set to graduate from college with an associate degree around the same time I was graduating from high school. If I waited for her to come pick me up, I'd be here for at least another three hours, and I definitely didn't want to be stuck in this hellhole for any longer than was necessary. It was bad enough we had to share the car in the first place, but her college trumped my high school. That, combined with the fact that we lived in a microscopic town in which the closest thing to public transport was an old farmer with no teeth in a pickup truck, meant that the school bus was the only other option for me. Now that it was gone, I was officially stranded and had no other choice but to walk.

At least it was sunny out, even if the early November breeze was on the bitter side. Grumbling under my breath, I pulled my hood up to fight the chill and quickened my pace. The sooner I got home, the better.

Pinecrest was a ridiculously small town in lower Michigan. I wouldn't be surprised if it came up under the definition for "the middle of nowhere." The only things we had here were cornfields and a dying downtown. Most people drove right through without realizing they had been here. Consequently, this meant that our school was too small to have all of the clichéd cliques. The largest class in the whole school, the sophomore, was only around fifty students. The only reason the class was even that big was because our school combined with another a few years back. As far as I knew, the other school had some financial problems and had to send its student body to Pinecrest so it could close its doors for good. Even though that practically doubled the size of our school, we were still small compared to most other high schools, and that meant everyone was involved in everything. There were cheerleaders who volunteered with the National Honor Society, jocks who were the lead roles in musical productions the drama club put together twice a year, and mathletes who played trumpet in the high school band. From what I could tell so far of the new guy, he'd fit in with any of the cliques.

It really made it difficult to create social boundaries, though there were still some who tried. I wasn't part of any of it, though. I hadn't jumped into anything when I was a freshman, and as a result, I always felt as though it was too late to join. Friendships were already established and I felt like I'd be intruding in some way. Besides, the only thing I was really interested in was cooking, but there was no club for that. I should probably be thankful for that, though. If there was, I would likely be the only boy to join, which would just give Morgan and his friends more ammunition to use against me.

In hindsight, I realized that I would have had a lot

more friends had I joined at least one club, but there was nothing I could do to change that now. It was already senior year. I just had to suck it up for a few more months, and then hopefully college would offer a clean slate for me.

I understood then that, in a way, Jordan was in a similar position to me. He was the new kid. Neither of us was previously a part of any extracurricular activities here and, as far as I knew, he hadn't joined anything yet. I guess he had an excuse, though, having just transferred to Pinecrest. I'd been here the whole time, so I didn't have an excuse.

Jordan was friendly and charismatic enough to join anything and be accepted with open arms. He made people laugh effortlessly, he was kind, he paid attention in class, and he was toned enough that he had probably been some sort of athlete at his last school.

I only hoped that he wouldn't turn out to be like Morgan, Nate, or Cole, because that would make for a miserable rest of the semester.

Ø

After what seemed like hours of walking by nothing but cornfields and dirt roads, I was relieved to finally reach my neighborhood. It was around twenty houses in total. They were all clustered on a few small streets off the main road, so it was sort of like a little suburb. I only knew a few of the neighbors, though my parents probably knew more of them.

Once I turned off the main road, it only took a few more minutes to reach my house. There was nothing special about it, really. It was just like all the other houses here: white picket fence, pale yellow paint, and dying flowers in the boxes beneath all of the first-floor windows that could be seen from the street. Well, the dying flowers might be specific to my house, since nobody in my family really took the time to take care of them.

It was a good neighborhood, though. We had lived in it for as long as I could remember and had never had any issues worth worrying about.

My mother had grown up in this area, though she had moved as far away for college as she could without actually leaving the state. Once she got together with my father and realized how many job opportunities were a reasonable distance away from her hometown, however, she ended up convincing him to move back with her, start a family, settle down.

My mother had a degree in mechanical engineering and was currently working for a company called Kalamazoo Area Research and Development. My father was one of the higher-ups at an accounting firm called Steinmetz and Happel LLC, which had a location up in Grand Rapids. I wasn't sure of his exact title there, but he made good money. So did Mom. With how much money they both made, I had no doubt in my mind that they could afford something less plain than our small suburban home in this small, boring town, but the location was what kept us here.

It took my father less than an hour to get to work every day. My mother and my sister could both get to Kalamazoo in about a half hour, and we were close enough to the high school that I could walk home if I needed to. So instead of using their hefty paychecks to find us somewhere more exciting to call home, my parents chose to live frugally and save up for our college funds and for their own retirement.

No one else was home yet—both my parents were working late tonight, and my sister wouldn't be home from community college for a couple of hours still. I tossed my backpack on the couch and plopped down beside it. It was only a little after four o'clock, so I figured I would watch a little TV before starting dinner for my sister and me. However, there was nothing good on, so I left it on a random channel and pulled out my smartphone to play a game before noticing it was down to only seven percent battery.

Sighing, I got up off the couch and made my way upstairs to find my charger. In my room, I flopped stomach-down on my mattress and reached for the charging cord, which was plugged into an outlet on the far side of the bed. Finding the end of it, I plugged in my phone and left it on my nightstand to charge.

Returning to the top of the stairs, I paused in front of one of the pictures hanging on the wall. It was of my sister, Eleanor, and me playing on the beach when we were around four or five. We were fraternal twins but back then we looked nearly identical. We were practically inseparable too.

Unfortunately, we had grown apart significantly over the last few years. Ellie turned out to be a lot smarter than I was, and while we were both sophomores, she had taken an exit exam to get out of high school early. The classes offered at our school were never a challenge for her, even those like calculus or Advanced Placement literature. She was eager to move on to bigger and more challenging curriculums, so she took a test that proved there was no use in making her stay and sit through lessons she already understood. Now she was racking up as many credits as she could at KVCC.

Apparently, she wanted to wait until she was the same age as the other incoming freshmen before she started university. Not that I blamed her—I wouldn't have wanted to be the only sixteen-year-old on a college campus either. We'd be turning eighteen in December, so we'd both be heading off to university next fall, provided I got into one. I was pretty sure Ellie would have enough transfer credits to have sophomore or junior standing her first year. I'd have a few transfer credits from my one AP class, assuming I passed the test at the end, but not nearly as many as her.

Speaking of which, I still needed to figure out what the hell I was doing with my life so I could decide which colleges to apply to and get my applications together. It was hard, though. I didn't like to think about the future. This was one of the biggest decisions I'd ever had to make and it was stressing me out every time I tried to think about it. What if I made the wrong choice? What if I hated my major and ended up wasting a bunch of my parents' money? I knew for a fact that they wanted me to go into something technical or business related, but I honestly didn't think I would enjoy that. In that sense, I felt like an outcast in my family—my mother, father, and sister were all heavily left-brained people, whereas I didn't like all of the analytical, academic things they did. I wasn't interested in being a mathematician, or a scientist, or a businessman like they wanted me to be. The only thing I knew I was interested in was cooking—which I knew would not make a stable career—and with the deadlines for applications coming up fast, I was running out of time to come up with a plan.

My dad had tried to sit me down and talk through some options a couple of times. He was a numbers guy, so he had the costs of a bunch of different colleges lined up for me on a spreadsheet to compare, as well as the point when I would have to decide on a specific major. Luckily, if I went to a liberal arts college I could spend the first few semesters taking general classes that applied to most majors and make an official decision on a major after those classes were done. Both he and my mother were encouraging me to figure out my interests now so that I didn't end up taking classes I didn't need in college. Honestly, I wanted to talk to them more about it. This decision could impact the rest of my life, but every time I tried to talk about it with them, my brain shut down and went into this panic mode where it was impossible to retain any new information.

I had spent most of my life eagerly waiting for the day when I could leave high school behind, but now that that time was actually getting close, I was realizing how terrifying the future was. I didn't want to be an adult. I didn't want to be responsible for such life-altering decisions. I just wanted things to be the same as they'd always been.

But unfortunately, that wasn't an option. I would be shipped off to some college or another next fall. I guess the military was always an option as well, but I couldn't really see myself doing that.

Feeling defeated, I trudged back downstairs, collapsed on the couch, and stuffed a throw pillow under my head. I closed my eyes and listened to television chefs pull together an easy five-ingredient chicken dinner perfect for families on the go.

I must've fallen asleep, because when I opened my eyes again, it was almost six. I contemplated going back to sleep for a little bit, but then decided I might as well start dinner before Ellie got home.

I hoped we had all the ingredients needed for spaghetti.

DON'T FORGET THE PARMESAN!

I turned on the radio in the kitchen and immediately started humming along to the Rolling Stones tune that was playing. I couldn't recall the name of it at first, but the melody was familiar and the voice was definitely Mick Jagger's. Once the chorus kicked in, the name suddenly clicked back into my brain: "Sympathy for the Devil." Though those words were never actually said over the course of the song, it was implied throughout. The lyrics cleverly referenced all sorts of historical events, retold from the first-person point of view—anything from the Bolshevik Revolution in Russia to the Hundred Years' War. I wasn't much of a history buff, but I enjoyed the fact that I could recognize some of the references. There were still a few that escaped me, but I could always look them up later if I happened to remember. Or maybe I could ask my sister. She usually knew about that kind of stuff.

I rummaged through the cabinets in search of ingredients. There I found two packages of pasta, some garlic-and-herb-flavored sauce, and a can of diced tomatoes. Then, while checking to make sure there was parmesan cheese in the fridge, I spotted some leftover sloppy joe mix from the other night.

"That could be interesting," I muttered to myself as I pulled out the sloppy joe mix and set it on the counter, thinking I could add it to the sauce.

Making dinner was my favorite time of day. Being able to pull together ingredients and make something for my whole family to enjoy gave me a sense of accomplishment that I rarely got from any other part of my life. Any achievements at school were overshadowed by the fact that my sister was doing better, but cooking was my thing. I was the only one in my family who was both willing and able to cook. I really loved being able to take things that you wouldn't normally think to put together and turn them into something delicious.

After washing my hands, I stooped down to look through the pots and pans. I had to shift some things around a bit, but eventually I was able to pull out a large pot for the pasta and a smaller one with a matching lid for the sauce. I held the larger pot in the sink and turned on the water. The pot grew heavier under the running faucet. I watched as the surface of the water inched higher and higher, all the while trying to estimate how much I would need to boil two packages of angel hair pasta.

Determining that I had enough, I shut off the water and transferred the pot to the stove. I turned the burner on to the highest setting and added a bit of salt and vegetable oil to the water to give the pasta a better flavor and make sure the noodles didn't stick together. Then, while waiting for the water to boil, I started on the sauce.

It wasn't long before I had everything going. After setting the timer on the stove, I pulled out a stool from the kitchen island and took a seat. I played with my hands, since there wasn't much else to do while I waited. I was starting to smell all the spices I'd added to the sauce, and my mouth watered in anticipation. I hadn't made spaghetti in quite a while.

I became lost in thought again and ran my fingers through my unruly hair as I went over all of the things I needed to do this weekend. There were a few pages of AP Chemistry homework that I had to finish, as well as some calculus. I was not looking forward to doing either.

The timer went off then, pulling me out of my thoughts. I slid off of the stool and turned off both burners before grabbing some pot holders from the drawer beside the stove. Then I gripped both handles of the pot and carefully transferred it to the sink, where I dumped the pasta into a colander to drain the water.

By then it was around half past six. As I waited for the pasta to cool, I stepped into the living room and looked out the front window. Ellie would be getting home any minute now, and I wanted to check and see if I could spot her car coming down the road yet.

I saw nothing, so I went back into the kitchen and dished myself up a plate of spaghetti. I was just adding the sauce to my plate when I heard the front door open. I perked up a little and turned to see my sister as she entered the kitchen.

"Hey, how was your day?" I asked as I set my plate down on the island and turned to grab some fresh parmesan from the fridge.

"A nightmare," she said, dropping her backpack on the floor at the bottom of the stairs. She tossed her car keys on the kitchen counter. "I've got three exams on Monday and I'm not ready for any of them. Is that for me?"

"Yeah, you can have it," I said. She wasted no time reaching out and dragging the plate of spaghetti closer to her.

"I've got to go study," she breathed. "Do you mind if I take this to my room?"

"That's fine," I said, though I was a bit deflated by the realization that I would have to eat alone again. She grabbed the plate with one hand and stooped down to grab her bag off the floor with the other.

"Wait!" I called. "Don't forget the parmesan!"

"Oh yeah." She turned and put the plate back on the counter. I handed her the block of fresh parmesan and a cheese grater. After she'd taken as much as she wanted, she disappeared upstairs. I got myself a new plate, doled out another portion of spaghetti, and sat down at the island to eat dinner by myself.

I couldn't help but notice that this was becoming more and more common.

Ø

It was around nine at night. I was sitting on the couch mindlessly watching reruns of *Friends* when I heard the first car pull into the driveway. A few minutes later, my mother came through the front door.

"Hey, Mom," I said as she shrugged off her jacket and hung it on the hook by the door.

"Hey, honey," she responded, a bit out of breath.

"How was your day?"

"A bit hectic," she said, placing her keys on the small table by the front door. "The deadline for that big project I've been working on is coming up. We've all had to work overtime to make sure it gets done on time."

"Ah. I made spaghetti for dinner. There's some in the fridge if you want it."

"Oh, no thank you, honey. I stopped and got a gyro to eat on my way back from Kalamazoo."

"Oh." I sank into the couch even more. "When's Dad supposed to get back?"

"He texted me earlier saying he had a late meeting with some clients. I suspect he's already on his way home, though, so it shouldn't be too much longer."

I nodded. "Okay."

"Did you have a good day at school?"

"Yeah," I said, not bothering to supply her with any details. She didn't ask for any either.

There had been a time in my life when she would've bugged me relentlessly until I told her something specific about my day, but I had always been stubborn, and after all the stress and exhaustion that came from work, she didn't have the energy to ask anymore. At this point, I was tired of being stubborn, and I would've honestly given her more information if she simply asked for it. But she didn't.

In all honesty, I missed her overbearing and inquisitive nature. It had at least shown that she cared. I knew she still did, but she didn't show it as much anymore.

"That's good." She nodded a little to herself, yawning.

"Welp. This project has me pretty beat. I think I'm going to call it an early night and head up to bed."

"That seems like a wise idea," I said.

She looked like she definitely needed the extra sleep—there were dark circles already forming under her eyes. I couldn't imagine the stress she was under. I didn't know the first thing about design, but I knew she had to work with a whole team of engineers from different disciplines to finish her project, and that was a lot for anyone to juggle.

When we were younger, before my mom got this job, she was more hands on, and while Ellie flourished with her new opportunities, I was feeling further and further behind. It was easier when I was younger. My mom would throw us both into the same activities—gymnastics, toddler dance class, various sports where I'd always sit on the sidelines—but as we got older, she had to work more, and everyone in my house got busier except for me. The idea that I was an island, here, making dinner, watching TV, getting to and from school, was harder and harder to change. I knew I should do more, but I just couldn't.

"I'll see you sometime tomorrow," my mother said.

"Okay." I watched her make her way upstairs to her bedroom. Then, when she was out of sight, I turned my attention back to the television. Dad didn't get home until around half past nine.

"Hey, kiddo," he said, walking in and spotting me on the couch.

"Hey. There's pasta in the kitchen," I informed him.

His eyes lit up and he immediately moved in that

direction. "Good. I haven't eaten all day. I'm so hungry I could probably eat an entire cow right now and still not be satisfied."

"I don't doubt that."

I pushed myself up off the couch and followed him into the kitchen. I watched as he pulled all the stuff I'd put away earlier out of the refrigerator and assembled his meal. I noticed he didn't put anything away, either, which meant he was already planning on having a second helping.

My father eyed the microwave hungrily as he watched his plate of pasta attempt to turn in circles. We had square-shaped plates, which we only realized after buying were not microwave compatible. Instead of rotating on the little tray at the bottom of the microwave, the plate turned until a corner caught on the front window of the machine and then reversed direction until it got caught on the side of the wall instead. This cycle repeated over and over until the countdown finally ended with a few shrill beeps.

Dad pulled the plate out of the microwave and smothered it in parmesan cheese. Then he practically shoveled the pasta into his mouth. I barely had time to blink before the contents of his plate had vanished. After taking his last bite, he went back to the leftovers and immediately created another massive mountain of noodles on his plate.

"You eat like a teenage boy before football practice," I commented as he put his plate back into the microwave.

"And you eat like a man in his fifties. What's your point, Son?" he replied, teasing.

"I'm just saying you might want to slow down before I have to call an ambulance."

"Trust me—if I die because of food, it'll be because it was your mother who cooked it." He laughed.

"I don't recall your cooking skills being much better," I teased, remembering all the times he'd used the grill to turn perfectly good burgers into bricks of charcoal.

"Hey, I can make sandwiches and pancakes like a pro. That's how I survived before you came along with all your cooking sorcery, and that's how I'll survive after you've gone off to college."

I shook my head, amused.

"Nice hoodie, by the way. You thinking of University of Michigan?"

"I don't know," I said.

"They've got a good business administration and management program there. You should look into it. I think that's one of the ones Ellie is applying to."

"Maybe." I shrugged. I watched him pull his second plate out of the microwave and take his seat again at the island. He ate at a more normal pace this time around.

"There's always Tech too," he said through a mouthful of spaghetti. "I'm pretty sure there are benefits available to you since both your mom and I are alumni."

"Yeah," was all I said, busying myself with putting the leftovers back in the fridge.

"If you wanted to do a business degree up there like your dear old dad, I'm pretty sure the Impact Scholarship competition is happening in February. That's available for incoming accounting, management, engineering management, finance, economics, and marketing majors. I may have missed some, since I'm going off of memory, but I'm pretty sure it encompasses every major under the School of Business. I think applications for that are due in January. I could send you a link if you'd like."

"Sounds good," I said.

"It's a really nice school." He tried to convince me. "It's got that small-town feel where everybody knows everybody. It's also really beautiful. They say it's one of the best places to be in autumn. There are so many trees that everywhere you look is worthy of being a painting."

"Don't they also get, like, thirty feet of snow during the winter?"

"Well, there's that too." He chuckled.

I'd had enough of college talk for the time being, so I changed the subject. "How was work?"

"Not too bad," he said. "I scored a new client today, so things should pick up back at the office. What about you. How was school?"

"Good," I said. "We got assigned new lab partners in AP Chemistry today."

"Did you get a good partner?" he inquired.

"I'm not sure yet. He's the new kid. I don't know much about him."

"Hopefully, he's not a slacker. I always hated being partnered with slackers while I was in school."

"Yeah, they're the worst," I agreed.

"Where's your mother?" he asked after a few moments of silence had stretched between us.

"She went to bed already. She had to work late on that project."

"Oh yeah." He nodded, taking another pretty large

bite of spaghetti. I noticed then that his plate was almost empty again. "I'm probably not far behind her. I've got an early day tomorrow."

I nodded again, realizing our conversation was likely going to end as soon as he finished eating. And just as I predicted, as soon as he had taken his last bite and put his dishes in the dishwasher, he was off to bed.

Having nothing else to do, I turned off the television and headed up to my own room as well.

ø

I rolled out of bed the next morning determined to find something to do. It was actually pretty nice out for a Saturday in November, so I went to my sister's room to see if she wanted to go outside for a walk or something.

I knocked on her door. "Yeah?" she called. I popped my head in to see her sitting cross-legged in bed amid a mountain of textbooks.

"I was wondering if you wanted to take a break from studying and go for a walk to the park with me?"

"I can't, Eli." She looked up at me, her brown eyes apologetic. "Calc II is kicking my ass. I've spent two hours on this last problem already and I still don't have the right answer. I need to keep studying."

"That's fine. I understand." I gave her a small, tight-lipped smile. "I'll be out back if you change your mind."

"Okay, thanks," she said before returning to the

textbook in her lap. I closed her bedroom door again and made my way downstairs.

The house was quiet, which meant nobody else was home. I went to the front door and pulled on a pair of sneakers I'd left there and a burgundy-colored sweatshirt hanging on one of the hooks to the right. Then I cut through the kitchen and went through the door there to the garage.

Ellie's car was the only one parked inside. Mom usually parked on the other side of the garage, but I don't think she had last night—probably because she was planning on making a quick escape this morning. I went over to the back wall and looked around for something to do. Our old bikes were back there, but they looked like they needed some air in the tires, so I decided against that. I perked up when I spotted an old soccer ball stuffed behind a few totes. I fished it out and set it on the floor behind me while I searched for the tote with our collapsible goal in it. I found it surprisingly fast and excitedly carried the tote and the ball out to the backyard to set everything up.

I hadn't played soccer in forever. There had been a time when it was all I wanted to do—I didn't care about anything else. Dad was really into it too. He helped me practice in the backyard, and we watched tournaments on television together all the time. But then he got that promotion at work and didn't really have time to help me anymore. I started losing interest after that, and when it became evident that all the other players at school were becoming bigger and better at a faster rate than I was, it all became too overwhelming. I hadn't played much since.

I plopped down on the grass and opened up the tote, dumping out all of the plastic pieces for the goal. I needed to figure out how to put it together—we had long since lost the directions, so I pulled out my phone and searched for an assembly guide on the internet. After a short scroll, I found a set of instructions in a PDF document for the same brand I was using. I didn't bother reading the text, choosing instead to follow the provided pictures. It took a good half hour or so, but eventually I had a suitable goal. I carried it to the base of the only tree in our backyard and set it up there. Then, hanging the old tire swing up in a low-hanging branch to get it out of the way, I started to kick the ball around.

It was therapeutic. I found myself having fun as I bounced the ball between my feet and kicked it into the goal. I pretended there was an actual goalie for a while and aimed for different portions of the net. A good three hours sped by before I decided I should probably head back in and get some of my homework done.

CONCUSSION

It had been a miracle when I was able to get out of taking gym my freshman year. My schedule hadn't quite worked out because I was in an advanced math class that conflicted with the gym time slot. Now I was starting to think it was a curse. Unfortunately, I still needed a gym credit to graduate, and instead of being stuck with all the freshmen for a class, I was stuck with all the athletic students in my year who needed to fill a credit hour and decided just to take another gym class.

Needless to say, I had some hard-core regrets.

I changed quickly, ignoring everyone around me in the change room and shoving my clothes and backpack into one of the lockers. Someone had stolen my lock last week, and I had forgotten to pick up a new one, so I had no choice but to leave my things there and hope nobody messed with them.

I smoothed down my shirt and entered the gym. A few guys were playing with a basketball they'd found laying around while others in the class just sat around talking. Seeing as the teacher hadn't arrived yet, I walked over to the bleachers and sat patiently. I'd gone to school with most of these kids since kindergarten, but there were a few newer faces among them. Jamie Carlson, a girl with long, straight brown hair and freckles, had come here during freshman year. Now she was super into the volleyball scene and had lots of friends. Kaitlyn Fisher had curly blond hair and was pretty involved in our school's chapter of the National Honor Society, as well as being the founder of an after-school book club. She'd started here at the beginning of last year.

Jordan was the newest student. He had dark-brown, neatly styled hair, and seemed to have a bright smile on his face every time I saw him. He stood off to one side of the gymnasium, engaged in conversation with Penelope Dunn, a small red-headed girl I'd shared classes with since pre-school. I watched them interact for a little bit. From what I could tell, he seemed pretty friendly—hopefully he would be an all right lab partner.

Mr. Mason walked in. The man had only been teach-ing here for about six years. He was on the younger side, as far as staff went, and was pretty much here to take over for Coach Hanover once he actually decided to retire fully. Hanover had been the gym teacher and a coach at Pinecrest for several decades. In recent years he had started handing off some of his duties to other people. Mr. Mason was now the gym teacher as well as the coach for girls' varsity and junior varsity volleyball. He was younger, fitter, and friend-lier than Coach Hanover, and for that, I was thankful. One year with Hanover as a gym teacher was enough to make you feel like you'd just gone through boot camp for the military.

Mr. Mason walked toward the center of the gymnasium with a soccer ball under his arm and whistled loudly, signaling us to stop what we were doing and gather around for instructions. I pushed myself up off the bleachers and jogged across to where everyone was accumulating.

"All right, kids," he began, his voice booming through the gym. "It's pretty nice out, so we're going to be having soccer tournaments outside today. Head out to the field. I'll split you into groups there."

Most of the class swarmed the doors leading outside. A few of us, however, decided to walk at a more leisurely pace to avoid the chaos. Mr. Mason studied his clipboard as he followed. By the time I reached the exit, most of the class was already outside. I was surprised when Jordan, just in front of me, paused to hold the door for me.

"Thanks," I said.

"No problem." He gave a friendly smile and, once I had my hand on the door, went jogging to catch up with some of our other classmates and continue the conversation they'd been having. I held the door open for the people behind me as well.

He was definitely a nice person. Chemistry shouldn't be too bad.

As we reached the middle of the soccer field, Mr. Mason started reading off pairs of names. "Oh boy," I muttered to myself when I heard my name paired with Cole Decker's. This was going to be an interesting class.

"Oh come on, Mr. Mason," Cole complained. I looked over and saw him standing with his arms crossed over his chest. "Can't I have a different partner?"

"No, Mr. Decker. You will be Elliot's teammate, and you will like it."

Cole sent me a murderous glare as Nate and Morgan snickered at him. The teacher walked off to pair up more people. I was just grateful that we were playing on the field today, where there was nice green grass to break my fall.

I shrank a bit as Cole approached me. "If you make me look like an idiot out there, I will personally kill you," he said, scowling at me.

You already look like an idiot, I thought. At least this time, I had the common sense to keep my mouth shut.

"All right, everyone," Mr. Mason called out once the class was situated. "As I said, today we are facing off, tournament style. There will be two games going at all times. One on this field, and one on the field over there," he said, pointing to the adjacent field. "The rules are pretty simple: try not to foul, and the first team to three points wins."

I sighed at the notion that I had to stay out there until three points were scored.

"First up, I want Decker and Goldman against Anderson and Hughes!"

Cole *and* Nate? Now I was definitely going to die.

Cole and Jordan stepped up to fight for the ball while I stayed back and tried to ignore the smirk on Nate's face when he glanced my way. I had a bad feeling about this and cursed myself as the game began. I wasn't watching, so I quickly fell a couple of steps behind as Cole did his best to dribble past both of the opposing teammates on his own.

Not that he'd actually pass me the ball or anything.

As it turned out, Jordan was a pretty aggressive and skilled soccer player. His fancy footwork allowed him to steal the ball from Cole a couple of times, only for Cole to steal it right back. I decided to run toward the goal in case Cole decided to shoot for it and missed, but unfortunately, Nate saw what I was doing and ran forward to trip me. He snickered as I fell to the ground, but my fall was enough to distract Jordan, allowing Cole to take a clear shot at the goal.

Since we'd gotten the first point, Nate now started off with the ball, with Cole attempting to block him. I took it upon myself to stand near Jordan in case Nate tried to make a pass. I wasn't at all surprised when the ball came flying toward us.

Jordan easily caught the ball by bouncing it off his chest and immediately started dribbling toward our goal. I rushed forward and was able to snag the ball from him when he accidentally bumped it out of his reach. I turned around and started toward the other end of the field. Jordan was on my heels, and I saw both Cole and Nate running toward the goal—and beyond them, a clear shot. I took it. The thud of the ball against my foot was satisfying. I watched as it soared straight into the goal without any resistance.

Cole pursed his lips, probably upset that I took away some of his glory. Nate looked positively murderous.

"Nice shot," Jordan said, praising me as he jogged around with the ball. I hung back as Cole moved to guard him, but at the last minute changed his mind and went to guard Nate instead. Frowning, I stepped forward.

Jordan smirked as he bounced the ball between his feet. He passed it quickly to his teammate. There wasn't enough time for me to block it, but I did my best to keep up with him as he ran down the field. It didn't take long for Cole to steal the ball from Nate; as soon as he did, I followed Jordan back to the other end of the field, where he was running to take position as goalie.

However, on the way there, something hard hit me in the back of the head. I lurched forward. In a panic, I reached out to grab hold of something. The closest thing happened to be Jordan, who was only a few steps in front of me. I got a fistful of his sleeve as I went down, but it was enough for him to turn around in surprise and try and help me.

Cole, of course, smugly caught the rebound and easily made another point while Jordan was distracted.

I hit the ground hard, wincing as the wind was knocked out of me, which left me sputtering like a fish in front of the entire class. It took a couple of seconds for my lungs to release. Once they did, I sucked in air greedily and started to cough.

"Hey. You're okay," Jordan said, comforting me by placing a hand on my shoulder. "Just breathe."

"What do you think I'm doing?" I snapped, irritated, though it didn't seem to have much effect on him. I clutched my head and groaned, engulfed by sudden pain, thinking I might've hit it on the way down as well.

Mr. Mason saw me on the ground and made his way over. He knelt down in front of me and asked me a few questions, like my name and where I was. He also made me follow his finger with my eyes before frowning and saying, "I don't think it's a concussion, but you should still go to the nurse's office to make sure."

Great.

"I'll help him there," Jordan said before I could object.

"Thank you, Mr. Hughes," Mr. Mason said. He stood back up and tried to settle down the class again.

"Come on," Jordan said, and held out his hand for me.

Still holding my thundering head with one hand, I took his with my other and slowly got to my feet.

If nothing else, at least I'd scored a point.

I DON'T LIKE BULLIES

Jordan and I left the field and walked the long way back to the school. When we reached the building, Jordan pried open the heavy metal door leading to the gymnasium. It had been propped open with a doorstop, as it tended to lock as soon as it closed completely, and I'm pretty sure it couldn't be unlocked from outside. Either that or it was so old that Mr. Mason didn't have a key. Regardless of the answer, we were able to get inside.

"Your name is Elliot, right?" Jordan asked as we walked side by side down the hallway. "Elliot Goldman?"

"Yeah," I said, holding the back of my neck with both hands to try and relieve the aching in my head.

"I'm Jordan Hughes," he said. "I think we're lab partners."

"We are," I confirmed.

"It's nice to meet you," he said, sticking out his hand. I shook it quickly.

"Likewise," I told him, closing my eyes. My body

swooped as my head swirled, and I wasn't sure I could stand up straight much longer.

"Whoa, are you okay?" he asked when I stopped to lean against some lockers.

"I'm fine, I just—" Everything was spinning. "I need to sit down for a minute." Jordan grabbed my arms and helped me to the floor. The contents of my stomach roiled and it wouldn't be long before I threw up.

"You don't look so good," Jordan said uneasily. "Do you need me to go get someone?"

"No, just give me a minute." I drew my knees up to my chest and held my head with both hands.

Jordan wordlessly slid down the lockers to sit beside me. He kept throwing me concerned glances. I considered telling him to stop looking at me like I was a wounded animal but refrained when I realized it would only worsen my headache.

"How long have you been bullied?" he asked.

"I don't know what you're talking about," I mumbled, keeping my head down so it wouldn't spin out of control.

"I may be new here, but I'm neither deaf nor blind. I can tell this wasn't a one-time deal. They've been doing it for a while. That Cole kid had a look of glee on his face when he took you down. That's not cool."

"Who?" I asked, trying to stall. This really wasn't something I wanted to talk about with a complete stranger. With anyone, really.

"I don't know all of their names," he said. "But every time we're in gym, Cole finds some way to make your life miserable."

"It doesn't matter. I'm fine."

"You're not fine, you can't even move right now," Jordan said. I couldn't tell if he was referring to my physical state or my mental one. "And it does matter."

"Why do you care so much?" I snapped. "You're a cookie-cutter popular kid. You've probably never had to deal with any shit like this in your life."

"You'd be surprised," he muttered. "Look, I'm sorry I pushed you. Bullies are the worst, and I don't like seeing stuff like that happen to people who don't deserve it. Sometimes I get a little carried away about it."

"It's okay," I breathed, leaning back and resting my head against the cool metal of the lockers. "I'm sorry I snapped. My head is killing me and it's making me more irritable than normal."

"No worries," he said. "Fresh start?"

"Sure," I agreed, and went to stand up. Jordan was immediately there to help me.

"You good?" he asked.

"As good as I'm going to be. We can't sit in the hallway all day in our gym clothes."

"That's true," he said, nodding. "Onward we go." He started walking down the hall.

"Jordan." He stopped and turned to look at me. "The nurse's office is down this hall," I said, pointing in the other direction.

"Right. I knew that."

"No, you didn't."

"Give me a break! I don't know my way around yet," he said, pouting a bit. However, it was quickly replaced by a bright smile. I found myself feeling a bit envious at how white and straight his teeth were. It must have been sorcery or something. I had worn a retainer for three years and still had a crooked tooth behind my top right canine. It drove me nuts.

The nurse's office was up ahead. "I can make it from here. You better head back to class so you can change before the bell rings."

"Yeah, I guess." He scratched the back of his neck and looked back down the hallway. "See you in chemistry then?"

"Yeah," I said, opening the door to the nurse's office. "See you." I went inside and shut the door behind me as Jordan made his way back to the locker room. I let out a breath I hadn't realized I'd been holding and looked up to see the nurse already watching me with her inquisitive green eyes. I gave her a small, awkward wave. "Hi, Lisa."

"Hi, Elliot." She acknowledged me with a tired but accepting expression and gestured for me to sit down. "What happened this time?"

"I took a soccer ball to the head and I think I might've also hit it on the ground when I fell," I said as I lowered myself gently into an uncomfortable plastic chair in the corner of the room. "Mr. Mason doesn't think it's a concussion but wanted you to confirm it."

"I can do a few tests to see if that's true. Do you need an ice pack or anything for your head?"

"Didn't my parents approve me for painkillers a while back?" I asked in a hopeful tone. I had convinced them to fill out some paperwork that allowed the school to administer certain types of over-the-counter pain medicines to me back when I needed them in freshman year. I had made up some lie about getting headaches all the time so they wouldn't worry or suspect it was due to bullying. I hoped the paperwork was still valid.

"Yes, I believe so. I'll have to double-check your records really quick, but as long as everything checks out, I do have some ibuprofen I could give you. How bad is your pain right now?"

"I have a headache and it's making me feel a bit nauseous," I mumbled.

She nodded, clicking with her mouse to select a few things on her computer screen.

After that, she administered a few concussion tests, including ones where I had to walk in a straight line, similar to the way police officers test drivers they suspect are drunk, and read some stuff from a sheet of paper.

"What's the verdict?" I asked once it appeared she was finished.

"Looks like just a bad bump on the head, no concussion. It should be healed in a couple of days on its own. In the meantime, I can give you some ibuprofen and an ice pack to get you through the rest of the day. I can write you an exempt slip for gym for the next couple of days as well."

"That would be appreciated."

Lisa disappeared to grab an ice pack and a glass of water for me from the kitchenette in the back room attached to her office. She reappeared a few minutes later and handed me both before grabbing some ibuprofen from one of the locked drawers in her desk. I gulped down the pills quickly and pressed the ice pack to my head.

"Thank you," I breathed. The bell for next period rang while I waited for her to scribble out a note for Mr. Mason.

"I'll write you a late slip for your next class as well," she said after glancing at my attire.

I glanced down at myself as well—it was obvious that I still needed to change out of my gym clothes.

"Thank you," I said again. Exiting her office, I waited for the hallways to clear up a bit before making my way back to the locker room. There was no gym class this period, so I wouldn't have to deal with anyone—a fact for which I was grateful.

I swore under my breath upon entering the locker room and finding my papers and belongings scattered around the room. Kneeling down, I picked them up one by one. By the time I'd reached my locker, my despair had sunk even lower. There, on the floor, sitting in a puddle of what I could only hope was water, were my clothes.

"Great," I mumbled, setting aside my ice pack as I stooped down and pinched the wet fabric between my fingers. I lifted the mound of sopping wet clothes, grimacing as liquid practically poured off them. After giving it a sniff, I was relieved to discover that it was only water. Hopefully it was from the sink or the showers and not from one of the toilets. Carrying my articles of clothing over to the nearest sink and dropping them in, I ran some fresh water over them just in case.

"Now what?" Even after wringing them out, I couldn't just throw them in my backpack. They'd get everything else in there wet as well.

Walking back along the lockers, I managed to find an

unused one in which to hang my clothes. If I left them over-
night, they would hopefully be dry by tomorrow. Knowing
they would likely be left alone if nobody knew who they
belonged to, I focused back on my other stuff. By the time
I put all my papers back into my backpack, zipped it up,
and slung it over my shoulder, I was resigned to the fact
that I was stuck in my gym clothes for the rest of the day.
Begrudgingly, I made my way to my next class.

Ø

English literature flew by quickly, especially since I'd spent
so much time in the nurse's office and the locker room.
Before I knew it, I was packing up and heading to chemistry.

Everyone was lined up against the back wall when I
walked into the classroom. I moved to stand beside them,
staring longingly at my abandoned lab seat.

"All right, class," the teacher announced. "As promised, today we are changing the seating to accommodate
your new lab partners. Please wait patiently until I call out
your names."

The teacher started directing students to their new
seats, which gave me time to zone out. It was only when
my name was called that I finally snapped to attention and
walked over to where I'd been directed. Jordan plopped
into the seat next to me and took out his textbook. I caught
him briefly glancing at my outfit, sympathy clouding his
eyes. He said nothing, though, and for that, I was glad.

Once everyone was seated, and after two or three tries
getting the class to calm down, Ms. Dailey returned to the

front of the classroom and began her lecture on how to calculate the standard deviation and percent relative standard deviation—or RSD—of a data set. From what I could tell, standard deviation was basically a measurement of how much our data points were spread out from each other, and the %RSD was the standard deviation compared to the average of the data. The concept seemed pretty straightforward, but the process of getting there was a little more complicated. I buried myself in my notes, doing my best to translate what was practically hieroglyphics in the equations into something more understandable. All the while, I had to ignore the concerned glances from the boy beside me.

"How's your head?" he whispered quietly.

"Fine," I muttered as I took down notes on summation. "It's not a concussion. The nurse told me to take it easy for a few days but said that it should heal on its own. She gave me some painkillers, so it doesn't feel too bad right now."

Apparently satisfied by my answer, Jordan nodded and returned to his own notes.

There was a tinge of darkness to the room. I glanced out the window and saw a blanket of dark clouds looming low in the sky. While a school bus full of screaming children wouldn't be the best thing for my head right now, I would need to suck it up if I didn't want to walk home in the rain.

Ø

There was nothing quite like the school bus to make me wish I had my own car. I understood the logic of why my parents made El and I share one, but it wasn't fair that the only time I actually needed my own wheels was when Ellie had dibs on it. It was frustrating. I could probably count the number of times I'd driven our car on one hand, and we'd had it since our sixteenth birthday.

I rested my head against the cool glass of the bus window as I tried to drown out the sounds of the elementary kids. Pinecrest was a kindergarten to grade twelve school. The junior grades were corralled in the west wing of the school so interactions between the younger kids and the high schoolers were kept to a minimum. We all had to ride the same buses, though, so there was no escaping the chaos and screaming and high-pitched excitement of the younger kids. It was as if they saved up all their exhausted energy for the bus ride home. No one could contain them—they bounced around from seat to seat, jumped up and down, and were rambunctious until the bus driver threatened to pull over if they didn't quit it. You know: calm, relaxing, exactly what you need when you've got a head injury. Maybe walking would have been better.

Having been forced to ride the bus for most of my life, I had a sort of truce with the small children. Back when I rode the bus more frequently, I used to bring a whole bunch of extra snacks so I could bribe them to sit down and shut up. Luckily, my sister was willing to drop me off in the mornings on Mondays, Wednesdays, and Fridays since she usually left for her morning classes at around the same time I needed to be at the school. On Tuesdays and Thursdays I usually got a ride from one of my parents. That meant I didn't have to ride the school bus in the mornings anymore, which was a blessing in itself, and since I wasn't a little kid anymore, I was allowed to walk home if I needed to. When it was nice out, I much preferred a peaceful walk to the chaotic cacophony of poorly supervised children in a confined space.

"Hey, Michael." I leaned forward and got the attention of the rowdy eight-year-old kid a few seats in front of me who was standing on the seat so he could talk to the kids in the seat behind him. His head snapped to me when he heard his name, and his large brown eyes were curious. "Do you think you could keep it down? I have a headache."

"Sorry," he said, and lowered his voice from an overly excited yell to a more normal volume. I knew he would get loud again in a few minutes, but it was better for now.

"Elliot, do you have any food?" One of the middle schoolers, a small girl with mouse-brown hair named Anne, asked me after a few moments.

"Not today," I said, watching as a pout formed on her lips. Rule number one for surviving a school bus full of children is to bring lots of food. They're always hungry. Once you realize that, you know how to appease them.

Once Anne disappeared back into her seat, I turned my focus back to the window. I couldn't really see much, since the rain was creating streams of water against the glass, but I could tell we were getting closer to my home. I was thankful for that.

About ten minutes later, the bus stopped in front of my house. I slung my backpack over my shoulder and stood to exit the bus. There were a few children darting across the aisle to switch seats whom I had to watch out for, but I was soon able to escape the big yellow rectangle of hell.

As soon as I was safe from the rain and inside, I went upstairs to search for some more painkillers. I'd already decided that I wasn't going to tell my parents about my head. Honestly, I didn't feel like it was a big deal since it would heal on its own in a few days, and I didn't want to call attention to something that didn't need the attention. It wasn't like this hadn't happened before—some random injury—but my mom had totally overreacted the first few times I came home with a black eye or a fist-sized bruise and called the school, which kicked off an even more intense time when Cole and his friends were even more pissed that I'd gotten them in trouble. They were better about hurting me after that—more psychological warfare than physical.

After taking some ibuprofen, I laid down on my bed to relax for a while. I plugged in my phone to charge and then used it to look up possible recipes for dinner tonight. Maybe I would start cooking after a nap.

HOLIDAY TUCKER

My head was back to normal by Wednesday, but I almost wished it wasn't. It had given me an excuse to skip gym class and hide from large, noisy groups of people like those found in the cafeteria.

Unfortunately, while standing in line for food, shuffling forward inches at a time, there was no more hiding for me. The people around me chatted with their friends, but I remained quiet, minding my own business as I reached for a tray.

The lunch options were less than exciting as I moved down the line. In that moment, I felt that the only difference between the school and a prison was the lack of bars on the windows. The first food option was chicken nuggets that may or may not have actually been chicken. I recalled that some boys in the class did an experiment to see how high the nuggets would bounce if thrown at the floor. It was well above their heads, to say the least. The second lunch option was a sad attempt at nachos. The small circular chips were soggy from being drowned in liquid cheese. Still, it was one of the more popular selections. The final option was pizza that tasted like cardboard and had the consistency of a cooked noodle.

Grimacing, I asked for the nachos and watched as the aging, short-haired lunch lady slapped a malformed mountain of them on my tray. I quickly moved on and grabbed a small packet of apple slices and half of a tuna sandwich that would hopefully get me by until I got home. Then I grabbed a small carton of chocolate milk from the refrigerated display and waited for my turn to read off my ID number to the cashier lady at the end of the line.

In the cafeteria, which was really just the old, out-dated gymnasium with picnic tables placed throughout, I looked for a place to sit. It was loud and chaotic. Every little sound was severely amplified because of the room's horrendous acoustics. All of the sound waves bounc-ing around the room just seemed to blend together and overlap until one sound was indistinguishable from the others. I was glad we had gym class in the newer gymna-sium, because if I had to endure the sounds of pounding basketballs and squeaking shoes in this environment, I might actually be tempted to kill someone. In short, it didn't help my head in the slightest.

Most of the tables were already full. Eventually, I spied an open spot, but just as I started to make my way over to it, someone else sat down.

With no other spaces opening up, it was about the time that I'd usually find a place on the floor or go sit outside on the bleachers and eat. A shrill whistle echoed above the din, and there was Holiday Tucker, staring at me. She gestured for me to come closer. I briefly looked around to see if maybe she was looking at someone else before making my way over to her.

Holly was alone, as usual. She was quite an intimidating girl, with a nose piercing, a tattoo, bright-red hair, and a punk rock persona, but she used to be good friends with my sister—before El left this place. They were still friends, but not being together all day every day had dulled their friendship a bit. Though Holly was known to show up at our house every so often, the same rift Eleanor was creating with me because of her focus on her homework was being felt by Holiday as well. Holly hadn't made many other friends since my sister left. She purposefully came off as uninterested in and above everyone here because she hated most of our peers and didn't want to get close to them. However, I knew there was a nice person underneath that outer shell, so she didn't scare me as much as she did other people. Still, I was curious about what she wanted with me.

"Sit," she said as I stood awkwardly beside the table. I slid onto the bench across from her and set my tray down, immediately poking my nachos with a fork to test their consistency. I looked up at her again. She met my gaze. "How have you been?" she asked.

"Good," I told her.

"Good? I heard you were in the nurse's office again on Monday." She raised a single, skeptical eyebrow.

"It was nothing," I assured her. "I hit my head, that's all. It only hurt for a little while. I feel fine now."

She didn't seem all that convinced, but thankfully

moved on to another topic of conversation rather than prodding further. "How's El?" she asked.

I shrugged. "I'm not sure. She likes to lock herself away in her room to study all the time. I suspect you've probably had more contact with her than I have recently."

"She can be like that sometimes." She turned her eyes to the laptop open beside her tray and typed in a few things before an outburst of loud laughter across the room drew our attention. Morgan Cook was joking around with a bunch of boys from the football team.

"You know," Holly drawled, her eyes still trained on Morgan, "I've learned some very interesting things about him recently."

"What kinds of things?" I asked, mildly curious.

"Things he would go to great lengths to keep secret," she said cryptically, tearing her eyes from him and looking at me again. "You know you're like a brother to me, right?"

"I guess so. Why?"

"I'm a Tucker. Tuckers protect their family and don't take shit from anyone. I don't like those guys or how they treat you. You say the word and I'll give them what they deserve."

Images of Holly going off on them like a rabid dog had me fighting a smile. She was fierce. She always had been, even before she'd dyed her hair and started dressing in all black.

When we were all little, Ellie and I had been pretty good kids. We didn't make trouble, we were polite, and we stayed out of things that weren't our business. Holiday on the other hand, was mischievous and got herself into all

M. MONTGOMERY

sorts of trouble. When she and El became friends, our lives were turned upside down. She taught El how to have fun, and I had been the subject of more than one of her devious plans during my childhood.

I had thought she hated me at first, but after she stood up for me on the playground when some older kids wouldn't leave me alone, I realized she didn't. She liked to torment me, yeah, but in the end, she always tried to look out for me.

She was still trying to, but this wasn't her fight. It was mine. I wasn't going to have her around forever, so I needed to deal with it on my own.

"Leave it be, Holiday," I sighed, taking a bite out of my tuna sandwich. "I can handle them."

"Whatever you say." She grabbed an apple slice off of her own tray and popped it into her mouth before turning back to her laptop.

"What are you working on?" I asked, taking a bite of a soggy, salty nacho chip and cringing.

"A computer program."

"Hacking into something?" I asked.

"There's not much else to do here. Boring classes with boring people. Only some of them are turning out to be more interesting than I thought they would be."

"Just don't get yourself arrested."

"Don't roll your eyes at me, you know I wouldn't dream of it," she said, smiling and typing away.

The clattering of a tray hitting the table was unexpected. When I looked up, Jordan was standing next to me.

"You lost?" Holly asked.

"No, just wondering if anyone was sitting here," Jordan said, a hopeful but nervous look on his face.

"It's open," I said, though I couldn't hide the confusion in my tone. Nobody ever sat with me *or* Holiday so why would anyone want to sit with *both* of us?

"Cool," he said, and slid onto the bench beside me. He appeared to feel awkward for a moment before deciding to address Holly. "I don't think I've met you yet."

"Holiday Tucker. You can call me Holly."

"Nice to meet you. Jordan."

"I know," she said, turning her gaze to her laptop again. He appeared a little unsure as to how to respond. She added, "Everyone knows. It's a small school and you're the fresh meat."

"Sorry about her," I said. "She can be a little blunt sometimes."

"It's all right."

"How do you two know each other?" she asked, looking between the both of us.

"We're lab partners," I said.

"I see," she responded. She grabbed her earbuds off the table next to her laptop and popped them in both ears. Holiday didn't like talking to new people, so I was pretty much on my own when it came to starting a conversation with Jordan.

I was never very good at that. Outside of my sister and occasionally Holiday, I couldn't remember that last time I'd talked to someone my age outside of school. I'd never been the type of kid to put myself out there. The sidelines had always held more appeal for me.

Now that I thought about it, I suppose I did have a few friends back in elementary school. However, we drifted apart significantly when I realized I was the only person putting effort into maintaining those friendships. As soon as I took a step back to see if they would initiate a conversation or invite me to join a game, the friendships dissolved entirely. I was bitter about it for a while, but at some point I accepted it for what it was and concluded that if I couldn't have a real friendship, then I didn't want one at all. I was still nice to people whenever we had to interact, but if they didn't show interest in me, then I didn't show an interest in them. Plain and simple.

That was pretty much how I'd lived my life since then. Unfortunately, being a loner made it easier for people to pick on me. Bullies didn't need much of a reason to latch onto a target, and being alone was enough. It was little stuff at first, like little jabs in passing conversation, but throughout the years it had grown into bigger things. Of course, some things I'd done contributed to it, and I knew that. Even though I wasn't close to anyone here, I didn't like seeing other people being picked on, so when I did see it, I tended to do things to attract the bully's attention toward me and away from the other kid. It made me a bit of a magnet, but to me, that was better than watching other people get hurt.

Speaking of which, Jordan was playing a dangerous game if he wanted to associate with me.

"You know, if you value your reputation at this school, you probably shouldn't make a habit of hanging out with me," I muttered, stabbing absentmindedly at my soggy nachos.

"Why's that?" Jordan asked innocently.

"I'm an outcast here. If you keep being seen with me, you'll end up one as well."

"Reputations aren't important to me," he said, shrugging. He took a bite of one of his chicken nuggets. "Besides, out of all the people I've talked to in the week or two I've been here, you're the only one who seems to be human."

"What do you mean?" I gave him a weird look.

"I'm the new kid. Everyone here is assessing me, trying to figure out whether they want to accept me into their friend groups or not. Every time I talk to someone, they put on fake smiles and overly peppy attitudes to try and convince me that I should be their friend. But I've only met one person so far I actually want to be friends with, and it's the one person who wasn't trying to befriend me."

"You want to be my friend?" I asked with uncertainty.

"I do." He smiled at me. "You're not afraid to say what's on your mind."

"Don't say I didn't warn you," I said, a faint smile tugging at the edges of my lips.

Jordan shrugged again and took a swig of chocolate milk. He swallowed then asked, "What do you like to do for fun?"

"I don't know. Cooking, reading, soccer."

He perked up at that. "You like soccer?"

"A bit."

"I used to play soccer at my last school."

"Are you planning on joining the team here?"

"Nah." He shook his head. "I went through it once before. I don't think I'll be going through it again."

"Probably a wise decision."

"Besides, it's senior year. It's probably time to try something a little different."

"Any interests?" I asked.

"Oh, I don't know." He sighed, stirring up the cottage cheese on his tray. "I don't even know what's here that I could think of joining."

"Soccer, football, basketball, Chess Club, Drama Club, Book Club, Guitar Club, Comic Club, Quiz Bowl, Science Olympiad . . ." I listed off what I could by memory, counting them off on my fingers.

Jordan laughed. "And which ones are you a part of?"

"I'm not really involved in anything school related," I admitted.

"Why not?"

"I don't want to be trapped here with these people any longer than I have to be."

"That's valid." He grinned.

"What do you like to do? Apart from soccer," I asked.

"I actually like science quite a lot. I used to be in Science Olympiad."

"What events?" I asked, curious, as I had read through a few of the event summaries during the brief period of time that I had thought about actually joining.

"Forensics, Mousetrap Vehicle, Wind Power, and Electric Vehicle, to name a few. I got first place in the first three and third in the fourth. That was my freshman year, I think."

"Cool," I said. "Where'd you go before you came here?"

"Hanover High in New Hampshire. It was a bit bigger than this school, but still small enough that you had a decent idea of who everyone was. It was pretty much on the border with Vermont."

"Why'd you leave?"

Jordan was silent for a moment. He stared down at his tray. "It was time for a change, I guess." He glanced up again. "What about you? Have you always gone here?"

"Unfortunately, ever since I was five. Thank goodness it's senior year. I don't know how much more of these people I can take. Thirteen years is *enough*."

"It'll be over before you know it," he said. "Any plans for college?"

"No solid ones," I said honestly. "I'm looking into culinary programs at some of the universities close by. Hopefully I'll get into one of them. Otherwise I'm considering not going to college at all, but if I decide to go that route, my parents definitely won't take it very well. What about you?"

"Engineering, hopefully. I'm thinking about chemical engineering, but I heard that's one of the toughest disciplines."

"My mom's a mechanical engineer," I said.

Holly chuckled at something on her laptop, which made Jordan and me briefly pause to look at her. When we realized it was nothing important, Jordan picked the conversation back up.

"Where'd she study?" he asked, genuinely interested.

"Michigan Technological University."

"I heard that's a good school. For engineering, especially."

"It is," I agreed. Right then, the bell rang.

"Well, see you in chemistry," Jordan said, and threw his crumpled napkin onto his nearly empty tray.

"All right," I said, doing the same. "See you then."

I stood up with my tray, briefly glancing at Holly as she closed her laptop and slipped it into her backpack. She met my gaze and smirked knowingly.

"What?" I asked, confused.

She heaved her backpack up over her shoulder and walked with me to the tray return. "Oh, nothing," she said, though the way she said it didn't make it sound like nothing.

"If you say so."

Ø

"Wow, it's really coming down out there," one of my classmates, Aiden, muttered as he leaned closer to the window to watch the rain pouring down.

I didn't have to look to know—I could hear it battering against the window like full buckets were being thrown at it. It brought with it an eerie sort of feeling. The sky was dark, the wind was howling, and the rain was drenching everything in its path. My mind wandered away from the lesson and got caught up in the sounds of the storm.

"You okay?" Jordan asked softly, nudging me with his elbow.

"Yeah, why?" I whispered back.

"You haven't written anything down." He gestured to my blank notebook page with a slight nod.

I glanced at his. He had nearly a full page of notes, and

from the brief glance I got, it looked like pretty important stuff. "My mind was elsewhere," I admitted. "Do you mind if I take a picture of yours?"

"Not at all." He slid his notebook closer to me.

I rummaged in my pants pocket for my smartphone, but when I finally got it out, I couldn't get it to turn on. "Damn," I muttered. "Must be dead."

"Here," Jordan said, and pulled his own phone out of his pocket. "Give me your number and I'll send it to y—"

"Mr. Hughes," Ms. Dailey said sternly. "I don't know what you've been told, but I do not allow cell phone use in my classroom. They are a distraction."

"Sorry, Ms. Dailey, I wasn't aware. It won't happen again," he said with a charming smile.

She easily forgave him, merely giving him a warning before continuing on with her lesson.

"Sorry," I said in a hushed tone. "I should've warned you that she doesn't like them."

"No harm done," he replied. "I'll just get your number later."

I nodded in agreement, finally tuning into the sound of Ms. Dailey's voice and trying to fit the rest of her words onto paper.

RAIN, RAIN

At the sound of the final bell, I hurried out the door and ran to my locker. Today would not be a good day to miss the bus, so I wasted no time in getting my things. The halls were loud and chaotic as locker doors creaked open and slammed shut all around me. I had just put my last textbook in my bag and zipped it up when I heard someone fall heavily a short distance down the hall from me.

I slammed my locker shut and found Walter on the ground with three idiots who couldn't leave anyone alone standing nearby.

"Ew," Morgan complained. "It touched me. Now I'm going to smell like a dumpster for the rest of the day."

"Yeah, why don't you watch where you're going, freak show?" Nate spat.

"I'm sorry," Walter mumbled, scrambling back up.

"You okay, man?" He took my outstretched hand and pulled himself up.

"Yeah, I'm fine," Walter said softly.

"Come on. We've got to get started on that project."

He looked a little confused, probably because there was no project, but quickly caught on as he realized I was trying to get him away from the dirtbags behind us.

"Hey, I'm not done with—"

I whirled around, facing Morgan, cutting him off completely. "I'm sorry, were you saying something? I don't speak moron."

He fumed at my words, though Cole betrayed him by letting out a muffled snort. After shooting a glare at his friend, Morgan returned his gaze to me, but I was already ushering Walter out toward where the buses were parked.

"Where do you think you're going, freak?" A hand on my shoulder stopped me from going any farther. They'd caught up with me, but my plan was working: they were more focused on me than Walter now. I motioned for him to keep going without me and turned again to face the trio of boys.

"I don't have time for this. I've got to get to my bus."

"You think we care if you make it to your bus on time?" Morgan asked.

"Wouldn't it be funny if he had to walk home in this shit?" Nate grinned at Morgan. "I bet he'd look like a drowned rat by the time he got home!"

Morgan chuckled darkly. "And this time, it'd be all of him that gets soaked instead of just his clothes."

Cole crossed his arms over his chest—he had a bored look on his face. "Come on, guys," he said, annoyed. "I've got better places to be. Let's wrap things up."

"Cole's right," Morgan agreed after a moment.

"Practice got canceled for the first time in forever. We've got to go celebrate. Nate, take his backpack."

"Hey!" I protested as he pulled my backpack off my shoulders. I held on to one of the straps, but Morgan twisted my wrist until I was forced to let go, and then he shoved me against the lockers on the opposite side of the hall from Cole. I bounced off them and rubbed my shoulder while I watched Nate empty the contents of my backpack onto the floor. Most of my papers slipped out of their designated folders, and unfortunately, a breeze came down the hall strong enough to scatter them over quite a distance.

"That should keep him busy for a while," Cole muttered, pushing off the lockers and standing straight again. "Let's go. I'm starving."

Waiting until they were a good distance away from me, I knelt down to gather my things off the floor. Cole was right—it was a lot to pick up. I had just gotten to the last paper when a pair of purple heels came to a stop in front of me: Mrs. Reed, my English lit teacher. "Come with me," she said, and started down the hallway. There was no way I was getting the bus now, and I shoved the last of my papers in my backpack. With nothing but a sopping wet walk home in my future, I stood to follow her, resigned to my fate. I hoped Walter appreciated my good deed.

She led me to her classroom and gestured for me to sit in one of the empty desks. Mrs. Reed leaned against the front of her desk and interlaced her thin fingers. I studied her in the silence that stretched between us, wondering why she'd asked me to come here. She was a very tall, thin woman. Her nose was pointed, and her hair was mouse-brown with a hint of silver starting to show through.

"Why am I here?" I finally asked when I'd had enough of the silence.

"Did you know I used to be fat?" she asked nonchalantly.

I raised my eyebrows without meaning to. "Pardon me?" I asked, voicing my surprise.

"I used to be fat," she said again. "The fattest girl in school. They used to call me Miss Piggy. They called me lots of things, actually. Fatso, oinkers, big bitch . . . so many things."

I looked toward the door, feeling suddenly uncomfortable with the direction this conversation appeared to be heading in. Confrontation wasn't something I was particularly good at handling, and as Mrs. Reed watched me with her sharp, analytical gaze, I shrank into my seat.

"Why are you telling me this?" I asked stiffly, wishing I was anywhere else.

"Do you know what I did?" she asked.

"No."

"I stopped eating," she said plainly. Staring down at my hands folded atop the desk, I couldn't bring myself to look at Mrs. Reed.

"Unfortunately," she continued, "it's something that stayed with me long after I left high school. It was extremely destructive to my health, but even after being hospitalized on several occasions, I couldn't bring myself to stop. Even now, I still struggle with it. It's something I will carry with me for the rest of my life." She pushed off her desk and walked around a little. "I wish I had the courage to speak up about what was happening to me when it happened. But

I didn't, because the world was different when I was a kid, and it was hard to admit."

"Why am I here, Mrs. Reed?" I asked a second time, wanting her to get to the point of the conversation. Nothing against her story, but I knew what all of this was leading to, and I just wanted to get it over with so I could escape the feeling of dread forming in the pit of my stomach.

"I want you to know that you can come here whenever you need to. This is a safe place," she told me. "It's important for you to know that there is such a space and that you can open up here about what's going on."

"Thank you," I said quickly. I wasted no more time, eager to get out of there, and grabbed my bag off the floor and jumped out of my seat, hurrying toward the door.

"I've kept you after," she called. "Do you need a ride home?"

"No, I'll manage," I called back.

"Before you go," she said, stopping me once more. "I want to know why you let them pick on you."

I looked down at the floor then, trying to come up with an answer—any one I could. But only one came to mind.

"If they're picking on me, then they're not picking on anyone else."

I didn't let Mrs. Reed get in another word. Despite knowing I was about to get soaked, I was outside in a matter of minutes, putting as much distance between me and that conversation as I possibly could.

With my head bent low, I jogged out into the rain. It was coming down hard. Like, I-might-drown-standing-up hard. In minutes my hair was plastered against my forehead.

But being wet was nothing compared to how uncomfortable that conversation had been.

I was tired of people weaseling their way into my business. I didn't want people to see my problems and pretend that they could fix them. Yeah, being bullied sucked, but I just had to deal with it for a little while longer, and then it wouldn't be my problem anymore.

It would be one thing if the people who saw what was happening did something to actually fix it. But they didn't. Mrs. Reed knew I was being bullied, but she wouldn't do anything to stop it. Lisa wasn't stupid and had no doubt figured out that my frequent visits to the nurse's office were the result of bullying, yet she did nothing to stop it. It was easier for them to ignore the problem than confront it because bullying was one of those things that, if it wasn't addressed—fully and frequently—it got worse.

In my opinion, if they weren't going to risk waging full out war on the issue, then they should just stay the hell out of it.

Racing against time, and not wanting the contents of my backpack to become completely soaked, I halted briefly at a stop sign and checked for traffic. A pair of headlights paused before the crosswalk. I quickly crossed so they could move again. As my foot left the road, I heard someone shout my name: "Hey, Elliot!"

I turned and squinted through the torrential downpour. The vehicle from which the voice had originated had definitely seen better days. It was an older Subaru, and it had its fair share of dents and rust for sure. The passenger window was currently rolled down, and through it, I could see none other than Jordan Hughes. He had to duck a little bit over his center console so he could see my face from the low car.

"You need a ride?"

"I've never been more relieved to hear those words in my entire life," I said as I practically dove inside his car, landing on the passenger seat. "Thanks."

I slicked back my sopping wet hair so that it was no longer dripping water all over my forehead. I sat my backpack on my lap and pulled on my seat belt.

"Where do you live?" he asked me.

"Take a right here, then go down the first road on the left and stay on that for about two miles. Then take a right at the traffic light. My house is about a mile and a half down that road."

"You were going to walk four miles in this rain?" he asked incredulously as he turned on his right blinker and drove on.

I shrugged, unzipping my backpack to check and see if my papers were still dry. They were a little damp on the edges, but they would survive. "I didn't exactly have a choice."

"What do you mean?" He waited for a car to pass so he could make a left turn.

"I missed my bus, my parents work until six or later, and my sister has dibs on the only other car."

"You have a sister?"

"Yeah. Her name is Eleanor, but everyone calls her Ellie."

"Ellie and Elliot?" He chuckled softly.

"We're twins," I explained. I dragged my hands over my face to wipe off the rainwater clinging to my skin before flicking my fingers toward the floor mat beneath me to get rid of the droplets. Then I wiped my palms on the dry upholstery of the seat since my clothes were already soaked and would be no help in drying my hands.

"You have a twin? How come I haven't seen her around school?"

"She doesn't go to Pinecrest anymore," I said, shaking my head lightly to myself. "She's insanely smart so she took an exit exam to get out of high school early. Now she's loading up on cheap credits at KVCC before she heads off to a real university."

"What's KVCC?"

"Sorry, I keep forgetting you're new around here," I apologized. "It's Kalamazoo Valley Community College. She'll be graduating in the spring with an associate of applied science."

"What's her major?"

"Business administration, I think. She wants to be in some kind of management position someday. It makes sense. She likes telling people what to do and she's very organized."

"Sounds like she's got her life together," he commented, his right hand perched on top of the steering wheel and his posture relaxed.

"Can't relate." An excess of air rushed out of my nose in some semblance of a laugh. I noticed that Jordan had cracked a smile, too, though he kept his eyes glued to the road. The windshield wipers were moving at full speed, and the crashing sound of buckets of rain battering against the glass was eerily peaceful.

"Is she your only sibling?" he asked curiously.

"Yeah," I said. "Though at times she acts more like a third parent."

"I can only imagine." He laughed lightly.

"What about you? Any siblings?"

"I'm the oldest of three," he supplied. "I have a younger brother and a baby sister. Andrew is fifteen, and Layla is three."

"It must be nice being the eldest," I said. "I'm kind of jealous. Ellie's four minutes older than me and she never lets me forget it."

Jordan glanced at me like I was out of my mind. "Do you know how much pressure comes with being the oldest child? I'm the one who has to be responsible and set good examples for both of them. I mean, Andrew is old enough at this point that he is beyond saving, but Layla still soaks up everything I do like a sponge. One slip up around her and suddenly she's screaming the eff bomb all over the house."

I had to admit, I was thoroughly amused at the image my brain conjured up of a toddler running through Jordan's house swearing and causing havoc at every turn.

The conversation paused for a minute and I sat uncomfortably wet in the passenger seat. It had been so long since I'd met someone new, someone who didn't already know anything and everything about me. It was strange, and surprisingly refreshing.

"You said right at the light, right?"

"Yes," I confirmed. Jordan flipped on his blinker and slowed to a stop.

"You must not live very far from me."

"Really?" I looked over at him curiously. "Where do you live?"

"That little cluster of houses a mile or so down this road."

"Huh," I sat back in thought. "I guess I hadn't realized any of the houses in our neighborhood were for sale. Are you liking it so far?"

"Yeah. I mean, we haven't been in the house too long yet, but it's homey. Not quite home yet, but it's getting there."

"Do you miss your old neighborhood?" I asked.

"Not as much as I thought I would. It sucked having to leave a few of my friends behind, but everybody has to move on eventually, you know?"

"Yeah," I agreed. "High school doesn't last forever."

"And thank God for that," he said with overexaggerated relief.

I chuckled. It was a relief. I thought it was only natural for everyone to despise going to high school. I sure did.

"This street, right?" Jordan asked, already slowing down as he squinted through the rain-streaked windshield.

"This one or the next one works," I told him. "All of these streets are connected."

Jordan turned on his blinker as the car practically crawled down the street. We both strained our eyes to see past the rain running like a river down the window, even though I knew exactly where we were. I felt like I knew everything about this neighborhood at this point.

Mrs. Perry walked her dog at the same time down this street every day, regardless of the weather. Mr. Lee waved at every passing car, regardless of its inhabitants. It was predictable. My parents loved that about this neighborhood. I found it suffocating.

"I can't believe you were going to walk home in this." Jordan reiterated his disbelief as he leaned forward on the steering wheel to peer out the windshield.

"Me neither. I'm glad you picked me up. I could've drowned standing up with how heavy it's coming down out there," I said with slight awe as I watched the street. "It doesn't usually rain like this."

"It reminds me of hurricane season back home," he muttered.

I glanced over at him. "I don't think I would be able to live in a place that experienced severe weather. The only real intense weather we get here is white-out blizzards, but I would take one of those over a hurricane, tornado, or earthquake any day."

"That's understandable," Jordan said. After a moment, he rapped his driver-side window with his knuckle and said, "I'm here."

We passed a white house, though I couldn't actually see much of it through the rain. If memory served right, it used to be owned by an older couple. They were the people who left out a bowl of full-sized candy bars for trick or treaters on Halloween. I hadn't realized they'd left.

"Cool." We pulled up to a stop sign. "Turn left here."

"My house is the yellow one coming up on the right," I said after we stopped at the next sign, leaning forward. I squinted to see my driveway through the downpour. "This one."

Jordan immediately slowed down and turned on his blinker again. Thank God there was a mailbox marking the end of my driveway, otherwise he might not have been able to see where to turn. He pulled in and parked the car. I gave him a grateful smile.

"Thanks again," I said. "I owe you one."

"No problem." He offered a warm smile in return as I opened the door and ducked back out into the rain. I practically ran to the front door. Once there, I quickly unlocked it, stepped inside, and closed it behind me.

It was obvious the house was empty. There were no lights on, and the only sound to be heard was the rain pounding against the windows, walls, and roof. I ran my hand through my soaked hair again, leaned back against the door, and inhaled deeply.

"Home sweet home."

DROP THE BASE

"All right, class." Ms. Dailey clapped her hands once to get our attention. "Today is Friday, which means it is time for this week's lab."

I groaned a little, wishing I could just take notes instead.

"Before we get started," she continued, "lab goggles on for safety."

That garnered even more groans. No one liked the school's lab goggles. They were far too old and scratched to see out of, and they always left ridiculous lines on your face. Regardless, I slipped off of my lab chair and followed the rest of the class to the goggle cabinet at the back of the room.

Once a pair of the uncomfortable plastic goggles was pressed tightly against my face, I turned and made my way back to my seat. Jordan plopped down a few moments after I did. The storms had finally stopped; the sky was now clear, and the sun was shining through the windows. It was deceptive, though. It looked warm outside, but I knew it would feel more like the autumn weather we were supposed to be having this time of year.

Though I wasn't the biggest fan of cold weather, autumn was my favorite season. I loved seeing all of the warm yellow, orange, and red tones. Unfortunately, the colors didn't last that long—but they were undeniably beautiful.

Coming out of my thoughts, I realized, again, that I had missed a bunch of the instructions. I hoped that Jordan had been paying attention. When Ms. Dailey finally handed out the lab worksheets and I saw that we had to do titrations, I groaned internally. I was not a very patient person, which did not help when doing titrations.

"Now," she continued, "it's important to remember that doing titrations allows us to determine the concentration, or the ratio of solute to solvent, of an unknown solution using a solution of known concentration."

"Can we get that in English please?" one of my classmates asked.

"You're going to figure out the ratio of powder dissolved in a liquid to the liquid itself by adding a basic chemical to it until it turns color. Get to work."

The room erupted with the sound of people shuffling out of their seats to get started on the lab.

"I'll grab the sodium hydroxide if you dissolve the potassium phthalate in seventy-five milliliters of water," Jordan proposed, already slipping out of his chair to grab his lab drawer: a plastic drawer for the built-in cabinets all around the room, and which every student got when they started a lab-based science class. It had most of the standard

equipment needed for labs, like beakers, test tubes, graduated cylinders, thermometers, and other things of that
nature.

"Deal," I said, looking down at my lab worksheet again
to double-check that I'd heard him right.

I felt a small rush of air hit me as he walked behind me
to get to the table of chemicals, and with it came a warm,
subtly cedar scent. The confirmation that he definitely
smelled better than Walter was a relief. Focusing back on
the task at hand, I read the first set of instructions.

> 1. Dissolve approximately 0.4 g. of potassium phthalate
> powder in 75 mL. of distilled water in an Erlenmeyer flask.
> Record the measured mass in grams of potassium phthalate
> powder used below.

After confirming the name of the powder, I grabbed the
conical-shaped beaker from my lab drawer and a bottle of
distilled water and filled the Erlenmeyer flask to the seventy-
five-milliliter line. Then I moved back to the table full of
chemicals and weighed out 0.396 grams of the white potassium phthalate powder on one of the analytical balances in
the corner of the classroom. After transferring the powder
carefully into the Erlenmeyer flask, I returned to our lab table
and wrote down the number.

The potassium phthalate hadn't fully dissolved yet, so I
swirled the liquid around for a bit. It was then that Jordan
walked up with one hundred milliliters of sodium hydroxide in a beaker and an empty burette. We worked so well
together, like we had planned the experiment in advance or

had been partners for years instead of just meeting a couple of days ago.

"Did you add in a few drops of the . . ." He paused to look at the worksheet. "Phenolphthalein?"

"I don't even want to know how you learned how to pronounce that," I said, looking back down at the worksheet.

> 2. *Get approximately 100 mL. of sodium hydroxide (NaOH). Clean the burette by adding a small amount of NaOH to the instrument and roll it to fully coat the inside with the chemical. Pour the excess from the burette into a waste beaker. Then fill the burette with NaOH and record the initial amount below.*

Jordan was in the process of doing that.

> 3. *Add 3–4 drops of the indicator phenolphthalein to the mixture of potassium phthalate and distilled water. The indicator will turn pink when the mixture comes in contact with the NaOH in the burette.*

I grabbed the Erlenmeyer flask and walked back to the table of chemicals. I used a disposable pipet to add in three drops of the phenol . . . whatever Jordan had called it, before returning to our table. By the time I got there, Jordan had already set up a ring stand to hold the burette upright while we worked and was cleaning out the burette with the excess sodium hydroxide.

I set down the flask and glanced at the worksheet again.

4. Clamp the full burette onto a ring stand, then twist the clamp at the bottom to release drops of NaOH into the mixture in the Erlenmeyer flask. Between drips, swirl the mixture around until the pink color from the indicator disappears and the liquid becomes clear again. When the pink no longer disappears, stop adding NaOH and record the final amount of NaOH in the burette below.

"Do you need help with that?" I asked.

"I've got it," Jordan said as he expertly filled the burette with the NaOH. I could tell this definitely wasn't his first time doing titrations. He fastened the glass cylinder to the clamp on the ring stand and wrote down the initial amount of NaOH before turning to me with a smirk. "I'll drip if you swirl."

I cringed and we chuckled a bit. "That sounds so wrong," I said, but complied anyway, holding the flask beneath the spout of the burette. His words had made my cheeks flush. When I looked up at Jordan again, I nodded and said in a dead-serious tone, "Drop the base."

Chuckling, Jordan twisted open the clamp at the bottom of the burette and allowed about ten milliliters of the base to mix in before he slowed it down to a steady drip. I swirled the flask around, and watched as the clear liquids briefly turned pink on contact before returning to clear.

"Remember, class. I want within one or two drops of the sodium hydroxide for the color to change permanently to pink," Ms. Dailey called out, causing Jordan to cut off the dripping completely.

The pink color lingered a little longer before

disappearing. Jordan started to nurse in one drop at a time. I looked around and was amazed by how much further along we were than everyone else. While we were already close to getting a fully pink liquid, others were still trying to fill their burettes with the sodium hydroxide.

"How many times does it want us to do this?" Jordan asked.

> 5. *Repeat steps 1–4 two more times. Record results for all three trials in the table below.*

"Three trials total," I told him.

"You should go ready our second trial then," Jordan said, gently taking the flask from me and swirling it around, our fingers brushing. He added in another drop, never once taking his eyes off the process and seemingly not noticing the touch.

Trying to keep my focus, I moved quickly to prepare another flask with potassium phthalate powder, water, and the indicator that I could not pronounce. When I returned, Jordan was still concentrating on the flask.

"It's so close," I heard him mutter as he added another drop. Then, as if by magic, instead of the color disappearing when he swirled the liquid around, it grew brighter and turned completely pink. "Victory!"

Jordan set the flask to one side and recorded the final amount of sodium hydroxide in the burette before refilling it and turning to me. "Ready for another round?"

Three titrations later, we found ourselves sitting in the hallway, awkward red lines imprinted on our cheekbones and foreheads as we did our calculations away from the chemicals. We were the first ones finished, and not even by a little bit. Many of our classmates were just beginning trial two, but we had nearly figured out the standard deviation and percent relative standard deviation calculations at the end of the experiment.

"You weren't kidding when you said you liked science," I said, breaking the silence.

"Yeah. I love anything and everything that has to do with it. Physics, biology, chemistry . . . I don't know why, it just clicks for me."

"I guess it's a good thing that I get you as a lab partner then," I mused as I finished up the final problem on the worksheet.

"Definitely." He grinned, showing off a pair of dimples as he glanced over at my page. "Since we're both finished now, do you think Ms. Dailey will let us head out early?"

"It's worth asking," I said, not really sure myself.

"I can give you a ride home again, if you want," he said, standing up and offering me his hand. It was warm to the touch, and felt comfortable—easy to grab as he pulled me to my feet.

"That'd be awesome, actually."

We walked back inside the classroom and handed our assignments to a surprised-looking Ms. Dailey. After looking over our work, she reluctantly let us out early. I laughed as Jordan and I walked together down the empty hallways. I never got out of labs this early. Or felt this happy afterward. It was . . . nice.

PIZZA

I woke up just shy of noon on Saturday. I stretched out in bed and took a moment to rub the sleep from my eyes before groping for my phone on the nightstand. I squinted at the bright screen, checking for any notifications. There weren't any important ones—just a few updates for games I hadn't played in months.

Eventually I rolled out of bed. I ran my fingers through my hair in front of the mirror to make it look somewhat presentable before making my way downstairs.

"Morning." My sister greeted me from where she sat at the kitchen island, typing away at her laptop.

"Morning," I responded, and rummaged through the cabinets for a box of cereal. I pulled out a box of Cheerios and set it on the island before opening up the fridge to grab the milk. "What are you working on?"

"An essay comparing the Great Depression to the recent recession," she told me.

"Sounds fascinating," I said, not actually that interested.

I pulled out a bowl and a spoon before pouring out the cereal and milk. I had just taken my first bite when my phone vibrated in my pocket. I fished it out to take a look. There was a text from an unknown number.

"Who is it?" Ellie asked.

"Don't know," I said with a shrug. I picked up my bowl and carried it up to my room. I set it on my desk, sat down, and unlocked my phone to see the message.

Hey, Elliot!

Who is this?

I'll drip if you swirl ;)

How did you get my number?

I ran into Holiday last night. We got to talking and then I realized I never got your number to send you those notes from the other day, so she gave it to me.

Here they are by the way.

Thanks

Anyway, I was wondering if you wanted to hang out todya

Today***

Hang out?

Yeah. You know . . . that thing people do when they're friends?

Right.

When and where?

Typing . . .

I placed my phone on my desk and started to eat my cereal a little faster. If he wanted to hang out soon, I still needed to shower and get dressed. I couldn't honestly remember the last time I had hung out with anybody outside of school, and the simple thought of it made a mixture of excitement and anxiety flutter to life in my stomach. My phone buzzed again. I glanced down at it as I ate another spoonful of cereal.

How does 1:30 at that park down the road sound? We could kick around a soccer ball or something?

Works for me.

All right. See you then :)

See you then.

Before heading to the bathroom, I stopped at the top of the stairs and shouted, "I'm going to jump in the shower!"

"Okay!" my sister called back.

I hopped in the shower, confident that my hot water supply would not be hindered by any laundry Ellie may have started. By the time I finished and had both dressed myself and brushed my teeth, it was nearing one o'clock. The anxious, uncertain feeling in my stomach grew stronger each time I thought about what I was about to do. Then an awful thought hit me. What if it was all a setup? What if he didn't even show up and this was all some elaborate joke to make fun of the kid who has no friends? I shook the thought away almost immediately. That didn't seem like something Jordan would do. However, the nerves didn't die down one bit, because something in the back of my mind kept reminding me that I didn't really know Jordan and it *could* be something that he would do.

"You're being ridiculous, Elliot," I told my reflection in the mirror. "Get it together."

Picking up my phone from the counter beside the sink, I turned it on and checked the time again, since I had already forgotten what it was when I'd checked a few minutes ago. Seeing that it was shortly after one, I quickly did some calculations in my mind. It would probably take me a good twenty minutes to walk to the park, so I threw on a sweatshirt before grabbing my dirty dishes and carrying them back down to the kitchen. I rinsed them out and placed them in the dishwasher, then dried my hands and jogged out to the garage to grab my soccer ball. It was a good thing I'd used it just the other day, or I might have had some trouble finding it.

"I'm heading out," I notified my sister as I made my way through the kitchen to the front door, soccer ball tucked under my arm.

"Where are you going?" she asked.

"I'm meeting a friend at the park."

She looked a bit surprised but didn't tease me again as I opened the door and walked out. It was a bit chilly, but the sun was out, so hopefully it wouldn't be too bad.

After walking for a while, I checked the time on my phone again: 1:22 p.m. I wasn't too far away, so I would make it on time.

I arrived at the park before Jordan, so I laid down in the grass and started throwing the ball into the air and catching it again. I did this over and over again, until I tossed it up and someone else caught it. Jordan came into view, smirking as he tucked the ball under his arm.

"Hello," he said.

"Hi," I responded, sitting up. "I brought a ball."

"I see that." He dropped it on the ground and started kicking it lightly back and forth. He kicked it to me once I was all the way upright. "Want to try a one-on-one game?" he asked.

"Sure," I responded. "Where are the goals?"

Jordan glanced around for a moment before pointing to a bench a short distance away. "How about the bench for you and that tree over there for me?"

"Sounds good," I replied.

And then the game began.

I dribbled the ball between my feet, attempting to maneuver around Jordan. It was tricky, though, since he nearly got the ball away from me a couple of times. He was relentless, and when the ball got just far enough from me that I couldn't easily control it, Jordan didn't waste the opportunity and stole it from me.

I swore under my breath as I lost all the ground I had made toward my goal and moved to block Jordan. I was successful in making it so he couldn't get past me, even with all of the tricky maneuvers he had been hiding up his sleeve. He tried to get around me by faking which direction he was going to go, but I was able to see his intentions and managed to steal the ball away from him when he tried.

He was caught off guard, and I was able to easily race the ball closer to the bench. In position, I kicked it into my so-called goal.

"Damn, boy," Jordan said, grinning and slightly out of breath as he watched me retrieve the ball again. "Where did you learn to play soccer?"

"I used to play with my dad all the time," I said as I dribbled the ball between my feet.

"Used to?" Jordan tilted his head like a curious puppy.

I shrugged, passing the ball back to him with my hands shoved deep in my pockets. I didn't really want to talk about my family at the moment. It wasn't that I was ashamed of them or anything, it was just that I didn't know Jordan that well and didn't want to bore him with my mediocre life.

"You're damn good at it when those assholes aren't tripping you."

"Thanks."

Jordan passed the ball back to me before we started another round. It was an intense match, which I somehow won even though we were neck and neck nearly the whole game. Now we were just passing the ball lazily back and forth in the middle of the park. I mindlessly passed the ball back to Jordan and he stopped it with his foot. He stooped down to pick it up and wedged it under his arm while placing his hand over his stomach.

"Am I the only one getting hungry here?" he asked as he pulled his phone out of his back pocket to check the time.

"I could eat."

"Are there any good places nearby?" he asked.

"Depends." I scratched my head in thought. "Do you like pizza?"

"Who doesn't?" Jordan asked with a slight chuckle. I couldn't help but nod in agreement. People who didn't like pizza were odder than Holly.

"All right. I know a place." Uncle Tony's. It was only a few minutes down the road—within walking distance of my house—and its pizzas were to die for. I had worked there for the last few summers, so I considered the owner, Anthony, and his daughter, Sierra, to be good friends. "Come on," I said, excited about the prospect of seeing them again. It had been a while since I'd last been there, and I had a feeling they were going to chastise me for being away so long.

"Where are we going?" Jordan asked with a curious expression as we got into his car.

"Just down the road. Take a left out of here and it should be the second or third place on the right. It's called Uncle Tony's Pizzeria."

"Oh. I've driven past it a couple of times, I think. It's got good pizza?" he asked as he started the car.

"The best," I said, realizing I had spent way too much time listening to Anthony pridefully boasting about his quaint little pizza shop. "It's where I work in the summer, so I've got an in."

"Always good to know the owners," he joked.

I nodded in agreement.

A few short minutes later, Jordan pulled into the pizzeria's parking lot.

We climbed out of the car at the same time and I happily led Jordan into the little restaurant. The smell that greeted us upon opening the door was absolutely divine. Closing my eyes, I inhaled the sweet scents of oregano, tomato sauce, and whatever the secret ingredient was that Anthony swore he'd never tell me. This place had always felt like a second home—somewhere I could really be myself. Jordan chuckled at the stupid grin on my face but brushed it off as a familiar voice boomed across the pizzeria.

"If it isn't the one and only Elliot Goldman!" Anthony grinned, spotting me from his place behind the counter. He opened up his arms as he moved around the counter to meet me and asked, "How have you been, my boy?"

"Anthony!" I smiled gleefully and jogged up and hugged the man. He was quite a bit taller than me, probably standing at a good six foot four, and his width only served to make him look even more like a giant when compared to me. "I'm doing good! You?"

"Good, good." Anthony looked over at Jordan. "I see you've brought a friend. Is it your first time here, boy?"

"Yes, actually. I'm Jordan. I recently moved into town." He held out his hand and gave Anthony a firm handshake.

"You've come to the right place," Anthony said with pride in his voice. "We've got the best pizza in the county."

"I'm excited to try it," Jordan assured him.

A timer went off back in the kitchen. "Oh, I need to

get that," Anthony said. "Take a seat, boys. Here are some menus." He pulled two out from under the counter and handed them to us. He also grabbed two cups so we could choose a beverage from the fountain machine before disappearing into the kitchen.

"Come on, Jordan," I said. After we got our drinks, I led him to my favorite booth and slid into the seat that had been unofficially dubbed mine. It was at the back, mostly out of the way of the chaos, and it had a window with a nice view of some trees, which to me were nicer to look at than traffic. Jordan slid into the seat across from me. I scanned through the menu even though I already knew what I wanted. My favorites haven't changed in all the years I'd been coming here, and since the day I discovered the Mediterranean pizza, it had been my go-to order. Ellie had always hated it because it had black olives on it, but that just meant there was always more for me.

"What do you normally get?" Jordan asked, looking through the laminated menu, sticky with the heat of the restaurant.

"It's called the Mediterranean," I said. "It's a thin crust with chicken, black olives, feta cheese, roasted garlic, banana peppers, and spinach on it."

"Sounds good," he said while continuing to peruse the menu. "Back home, the only pizza places were chains or really expensive restaurants. Nothing homespun like this, with this kind of warm, inviting atmosphere."

"Yeah. Anthony has put a lot of effort into keeping it that way."

"You seem to know him pretty well," Jordan said, setting down his menu.

"I've been working here for the last three summers," I explained. "And I've been a customer even longer than that."

"That makes sense." His eyes flicked to the kitchen doors as they were pushed open.

Sierra came out to work the counter while her father stayed in the kitchen. She waved when she saw me. I smiled, waving back.

"Who's that?" Jordan asked.

"That's Anthony's daughter, Sierra. She's twenty-something and has worked here for as long as I've been coming here."

"She's pretty," he said disinterestedly as he twirled his straw around in his drink.

"I guess." I shrugged. I'd never really thought about it. She had long black hair and nicely tanned skin, but I had always considered her to be more like a sister than anything. We had grown close over the summers I had spent working here. We had inside jokes and silly competitions galore. I swear I spent more time here laughing than I actually spent working. I frowned when I realized I'd been closer to Sierra over the past few years than I had been to my actual sister.

"So," Jordan said, trailing off while continuing to stir his drink. "You got a girlfriend or anything?"

I snorted, which made Jordan look up. "Do I look like the sort of guy who can get a girlfriend?" I asked.

"It's not like you're unattractive or anything," he said casually.

"I've been targeted by the bullies at school for years.

Granted, I make it worse for myself by purposefully aggravating them, but at least that keeps their focus away from everyone else. They don't bully me because I'm a nerd, or because I'm too weird or anything, but everyone still assumes there's a reason and that if they associate with me too much, they could be dragged into it. Dating me is basically social suicide. So is trying to be my friend. I don't blame people for not wanting that. I wouldn't blame you if you didn't want that, either, but for some godforsaken reason, you seem pretty determined to be my friend."

The bullying caught up to me quickly one day in second grade, and continued on from there. I wish I could pinpoint why or how it started, but it was often the usual kid things—name-calling on the playground or being picked last for team sports—and without my sister there to put herself between me and guys like Morgan and Cole, high school was now a war zone.

Jordan shrugged and stared into his drink once more. "You seem like a pretty good guy to me."

"Thanks," I said, but I was unable to hide the bitterness in my tone.

"I mean it," he said, looking back up at me.

A weird feeling overtook me then. Something I couldn't identify exactly, but it was enough for me to want to stand. "I'm going to go put in our orders. You wanted to try the Mediterranean, right?"

"Yeah," Jordan said, watching as I stood, grabbed the menus, and walked over to where Sierra stood behind the counter. I briefly glanced back to see him gazing out the window, seemingly lost in thought. Doing my best to ignore the sensation, I handed Sierra our menus and quickly recited our order.

I would probably feel more like myself once I got a little food in me.

BOYFRIEND?

Over the next couple of weeks, Jordan and I grew a lot closer. He was probably the only real friend I'd ever had, and for the first time in a long time, I didn't feel alone. Whenever I was with him, I felt somehow lighter, happier even, and I think it was starting to show. Ellie had mentioned it the other night—she said I was smiling more. I hadn't noticed it myself, but thinking back on it, I suppose I had been.

It was Monday now, and I hummed lightly to myself as I walked down the hallway to get my stuff from my locker after chemistry. Ms. Dailey had started keeping Jordan after class every day to catch him up on what he had missed from the beginning of the year. He probably already knew most of the stuff, given his enthusiasm for the subject, but it was important for him to be fully prepared for any topics that may appear on the AP test at the end of the year—if he intended to get a high enough score for college credit, at least.

M. MONTGOMERY

I looked up then and was unlucky enough to spot Morgan, Nate, and Cole coming my way. I tried to duck into an empty classroom before they spotted me, but unfortunately, the door was locked. They cornered me before I had time to try another.

"Look what we found, boys. A little freak," Morgan sneered, with his arms crossed over his chest.

"Why do you always seem so surprised to see me?" I asked. "You do know we go to the same school, right? And that we all get out of class at the same time? And that we've been going to school together for our *entire childhoods*?"

"You'd be wise to shut up, Goldman. I've been dying to punch something for days, and your boyfriend isn't here to protect you right now," he growled.

Boyfriend? Where the hell did that come from? "What the hell are you talking about?" I asked, confused.

"That Hughes kid." Nate rolled his eyes as if I was the stupid one. "We all know you're fucking him."

"No, I'm not," I protested.

I took a step back from them, confused. Was that what everyone thought?

"Hey, take it easy, guys," Cole said, putting his hands on his friends' shoulders.

"Sorry, he's obviously the one screwing you." Nate smirked, ignoring his friend.

"You asshole!" I growled, and was unable to stop myself from throwing a punch. My fist exploded with pain as it made contact with Nate's jaw. It wasn't at all like in the movies. I shook my hand out while backing away, the realization of what I'd just done filling my heart with fear. I tried to run, but Morgan reached out, catching the back of my shirt in his fist. He hauled me back and shoved me hard into the row of lockers. I groaned, pain surging through the back of my skull and creating blue and purple explosions behind my closed eyes.

"Is that the sound you make for your *boyfriend*?"

An angry Nate had recovered from my punch and seemed adamant about returning the favor. Morgan held me in place as Nate punched me square in the face. I heard a crack at the same time that an indescribable pain sprouted throughout my nose. All my breath escaped me as he landed another blow, this time to my stomach.

"Guys, stop. Someone will see," Cole said, attempting to be the voice of reason.

"You're right," Morgan said, hatred gleaming in his eyes. "Let's take him around back where no one will catch us." He wrenched me forward, still clutching my shirt. As I struggled to free myself, Morgan and Nate grabbed my upper arms and dragged me through one of the back doors not far from my locker. School was already out for the day, so there weren't many people left to see us anyway. It wasn't worth calling for help. My best chance was to try to reason with them.

"Guys . . ." I tried to get their attention, but they continued to drag me until we were out of sight, away from any potential prying eyes. "Guys! Is there no opportunity for diplomacy?"

"Shut it, Goldman." Morgan released his hold on me and my left side dropped heavily onto the concrete. My elbow scraped against the rough surface and the pain caught me off guard. A hiss escaped my lips before I could hold it back. Nate let me go shortly after Morgan, and I fell the rest of the way to the ground, grunting in pain.

"Hold him," Morgan instructed, and then Nate yanked me up by my arm again. Morgan punched me in the stomach again. I tried to pull away from Nate, but his grip on my arm was so tight it was going to bruise. Morgan landed another punch to my stomach before Cole stepped in front of him.

"That's enough," he said.

"Get out of the way," Morgan growled.

"I said that's enough!" Cole yelled, pointing down at me. "Look at him!"

Morgan's eyes snapped down to me. I was sure I looked pitiful, hunched over with a trail of blood from Nate's earlier punch still trickling from my nose. Morgan was icily quiet as Nate finally released his hold on my arm and I collapsed on the ground.

"Let's go," Morgan grumbled, walking away. Nate followed. Cole was the last to go, but before leaving, he looked down at me. I glanced up at him, unable to see much more than his figure through my disorientation and the tears pooling in my eyes. Wordlessly, he too walked away.

I closed my eyes, too sore to pick myself back up again. Not yet. Maybe if I just laid here for a few minutes, my body would stop burning.

Ø

A shrill noise pierced my subconscious, giving me another

shock to my system. I peeled open my heavy eyelids despite the brightness of the sun. I heard the sound again—it caused me to wince. Sluggishly, I realized that the noise was my cell phone.

I slowly reached into my pocket and, ignoring the stinging pain the movement caused, pulled out my phone just as the caller ID disappeared and the call dropped. I swore and let my arm fall slack. The surface beneath me was hard and uncomfortable, but I still couldn't bring myself to stand up.

My phone went off again, and this time I saw who it was: Jordan. I slid my finger across the screen and winced as I brought it to my ear. "Jordan?"

"Hey, where are you?" he breathed. "I've looked everywhere."

"Outside," I hissed, accidentally breathing too deeply. The bruises quickly forming on my ribs shrieked in protest. "Around the back of the school, where the east side faces the trees. There's a small parking lot that nobody uses because none of the doors back here are accessible from the outside. I'm between the loading dock for the cafeteria and one of the dumpsters."

"Are you okay?" I could hear the concern in his voice. "What happened? You sound hurt."

"Come get me," I mumbled, too exhausted to carry on the conversation.

"I'm on my way," he said, and ended the call.

I dropped my arm again and closed my eyes. Everything hurt. I was on the edge of falling asleep again when the sound of shoes jogging across the pavement woke me.

M. MONTGOMERY

"Elliot?" Jordan dropped to his knees beside me. "What happened?" he asked, worried. "Who did this?" He gently placed his hand on my arm as he looked down at me, assessing my injuries.

"They cornered me," I mumbled. "I punched Nate in the face. I shouldn't have done that."

Jordan's lips pressed together in a thin line. "Come on." He urged me to sit up. "I'm taking you to the hospital."

"No," I protested. "Home. Take me home."

"Eli." I could tell from the way his voice gave way that he was not happy with my choice.

"Home," I reiterated. I didn't care what he thought; I didn't want to go to the hospital. I could handle . . . whatever this was.

Jordan sighed. "Can you stand?"

"I think so," I said, holding out my arm. "Help me up."

Jordan looped his arm under mine and then around my back. He put his other arm under my knees and lifted me up so that my feet could find the ground again. I slung my arm over his shoulders for support. He braced me with a hand around my waist and walked me back to his car.

"I'm going to kill them," he said as he helped me into the passenger's seat.

I smiled softly, despite the pain. It was nice having someone who cared so much. "Holly might beat you to it," I said, leaning my head back as he climbed into the driver's seat.

"As long as they get what they deserve, I'll be happy." He put his key in the ignition and started the car. I said nothing, watching the world pass me by as we traveled down the road for a while. I closed my eyes again.

KISS IT BETTER

"Fuck, that hurts!" I hissed as Jordan prodded at the bridge of my nose. I was sitting on the edge of the sink in the upstairs bathroom of my house as Jordan assessed my injuries. For the first time in a long time, I was thankful no one else was home. My usual feelings of loneliness or even boredom had been replaced with worry about what my parents or sister might do if they came home and saw my face battered and raw.

"Sorry." He stepped to the side and wet a washcloth with warm water from the faucet. Stepping in front of me again, he anchored my chin with his hand and gingerly blotted away the dried blood under my nose. Once he had cleaned it all, he rinsed the cloth, wrung it out, and left it hanging over the edge of the sink to dry.

Jordan turned his attention back to my nose. "I think it's broken," he said, the pity clear in his eyes.

"My nose or my pride?" I asked nonchalantly, trying to lighten the mood a little.

"Your nose." Jordan chuckled.

"Why are you looking at me like that?" I narrowed my eyes at him, suspicious of his concern.

He nervously scratched the back of his neck. "I need to put it back in place." He stared at me apologetically.

My eyes widened upon realizing what he meant and that it entailed a hell of a lot more pain. I slid off the counter and backed away from him. "Absolutely not." I raised a warning finger at him as he stepped closer. "Don't even think about it."

"Eli," he said impatiently.

"No. No one less than a trained professional is touching my nose. I swear to God, Jordan, if you touch me, I will kill you."

"I've fixed plenty of noses. I know what I'm doing," he reasoned.

"What do you mean?" I asked. That was not a normal thing for a person to say. He had to be lying to try to make me feel better about the situation or something.

Jordan merely shrugged, offering up no additional information about his apparent *expertise* in fixing broken noses. I shook my head in disbelief.

"Definitely not."

"Eli—"

"I said no."

"Then you'll just have to explain to your parents how you got a broken nose and have *them* take you to the hospital."

We were at a standoff. After a few moments, I gave in.

"How many noses?"

"Hm?"

"How many noses have you reset?"

"Three," he said. "All successful."

"Are you lying to me?" I asked, my voice stiff with skepticism. "And how? I mean, why?"

"I am not." He held my gaze confidently and then softened it as he continued. "I had some friends at my old school who were bullied a lot too. One of them, Carson, was adamant about keeping it a secret from his parents. The first time he broke his nose, he made me reset it. And the second. The third time was on Drew because he was an idiot and sprinted face-first into a sliding glass door."

I regarded him carefully, trying to discern if he was telling the truth or not. After a short staring contest between the two of us, I sighed and stepped closer. "Fine."

Jordan closed the remaining distance between us and gingerly placed his thumbs on either side of my nose. "Okay. On three," he said, looking directly into my eyes.

I grabbed his wrists as if to stop him and scowled again. "If you do that douche-bag counting thing, I will kill you."

"What douche-bag counting thing?" he asked.

"You know, that thing where they go one, two—"

CRACK.

Pain. Searing, almost indescribable pain shot through my entire face as if a bolt of lightning had suddenly jumped out of the sky and struck me. It was like every nerve in my body was on fire, with the bridge of my nose being the epicenter of white-hot burning pain. I wrenched myself from Jordan's grip and collapsed to the floor. I screamed a string of profanities, every single one that I knew, in just one breath, and cupped my nose, wanting to curl up in pure agony.

"All better." Jordan chuckled and crouched down beside me.

"Screw you!" I screeched and backhanded him in the chest.

"Want me to kiss it better?" he cooed as if he was talking to a small child.

"Fuck off, Jordan." I rolled away from him and stood back up, staring into the mirror behind the sink. I gingerly prodded at my nose again, only to wince at its newfound tenderness.

"You're going to want to ice that," he said, appearing behind me.

"No shit!" I snapped without even glancing at him. He didn't deserve my attention, not after that little stunt. It hurt more than it did when Nate broke it in the first place.

"How are your other injuries?" he asked.

"Sore as all hell," I grumbled. I reached into the cabinet to my left and pulled out a bottle of ibuprofen. I threw back my head and swallowed the pills dry.

"May I see them?" he asked, staring at me in the mirror, his eyes dropping to my torso.

"They're fine, Jordan." I sighed.

"I still want to see them," he pushed.

I rolled my eyes and turned toward him, lifting my shirt a bit. I looked down at my bruises, not exactly sure how much damage had been done. They were mostly red and sore, but a few areas around my ribs had started to darken.

"It'll be worse in the morning," he said solemnly, still staring at them. "The bruises will have finished forming by then."

I dropped my shirt and looked into the mirror again. "It's never been this bad before," I mumbled to myself before catching Jordan's gaze—his eyes holding mine.

"What made you punch him?" he asked.

I shrugged noncommittally. "He said some stuff."

"What kind of stuff?" he pressed.

I turned and faced him again. "Stuff about us."

"Like?" He urged me to continue. In all honesty, I didn't really want to, but he deserved to know—in case they came after him too.

"He accused us of sleeping together, though his words were a bit nastier than that." I looked away, avoiding his stare. The silence between us stretched on for a while, and I couldn't think of anything to say to break it. Fortunately, Jordan beat me to it.

"I'm so sorry, Eli," he said, defeated.

I glanced at him again. His hands were in his pockets and he was staring down at his shoes. "I don't understand. What do you have to be sorry about?" I asked, confused.

"Everything. All of this. It's my fault they beat you up," he said miserably.

"No, it's not," I said immediately, denying his statement. "Those assholes have been beating me up since before my sister left school. When they started picking on her because she was smarter than everyone else, I did everything I could to make myself the target instead of her. I did it to keep her safe. Now I do it to keep other people safe." I paused. "If they're beating me up, then they can't hurt anyone else."

"But you said it's never been this bad before," Jordan said, looking worried. "It was worse because they thought you were gay. That's my fault."

"If anything, it's my fault," I argued. "I'm the weak, scrawny kid who's never had a friend in his life, and the only logical reason anyone like you would hang out with me would be to—" I couldn't bring myself to finish that sentence. "I'm sorry you got dragged into this."

"Eli . . ." Jordan said.

I shook my head. "They're just a bunch of judgmental pricks who can't keep their tempers in check. It's their fault." I folded my arms. "And who are they to judge us like that? Even if it was true, doesn't everybody have the right to love who they want? Why do they get to decide what's right and wrong? They're just a bunch of prejudiced assholes making assumptions where none belong."

Jordan finally looked back up at me. "Do you really think that?"

"Of course." I shrugged, my tone softening. "People are people, no matter who they love." I glanced at Jordan then. I couldn't identify the look in his eyes, but he seemed deep in thought. "It doesn't matter now, though," I continued, looking away again. "They're going to think what they want. I warned you about being dragged into this, about the risks of being friends with me. Now everyone is going to think we're gay even though—"

I was cut off suddenly by warm lips pressed into mine. They were slightly chapped but gentle, and they somehow made that funny feeling appear in my stomach again. It was nice at first, but as soon as my brain realized what was happening, that warm feeling within me bled into an icy panic.

I pushed Jordan away, too stunned to do anything but stare at the collar of his shirt. I couldn't even form a coherent thought.

"I told you I wasn't so cookie cutter," he said softly, backing away, shoving his hands back into his pockets.

I couldn't think of a single thing to say.

Jordan offered a weak smile in response to my silence. "I should head home. My mom is probably wondering where I am," he explained softly, not making eye contact. "I hope you feel better soon, Elliot."

He left then, leaving me frozen in place. Once I was sure he was gone, I gingerly brought my fingers up to my lips.

He'd kissed me.

Jordan Hughes had kissed me.

OH GOD

I laid in my bed with my eyes closed and an ice pack perched atop my nose. Though it had been hours since Jordan had popped it back into place, it still felt as though it was on fire. My whole body felt that way, really, but my nose was the focus of the pain.

I sighed. At least he had been kind enough to provide me with a distraction.

I opened my eyes and stared up at my blank white ceiling, but all I could see was him. The kiss played over and over again in my mind, whether I wanted it to or not. The memory was vivid. Each time it replayed, it was as if he was right in front of me. If I thought about it hard enough, I could even feel my lips start to tingle at the memory of it—the gentle pressure of his lips against my own.

I shook my head, trying to rid myself of that train of thought. I wasn't gay, so why did I feel so conflicted about this? Maybe it was because Jordan was the closest thing

I'd ever had to a best friend, and now that he'd kissed me, everything was different.

Or was it? I wasn't sure. But even as I thought about it, I couldn't help but picture his bluish-green eyes, his chocolaty-brown hair, which looked as soft as a feather. I pictured his dimples as he smiled, the way his eyes lit up at the mere mention of something he loved. I pictured his protective-ness, his kindness, his thoughtfulness. I pictured him.

God, why did he have to kiss me? I wasn't gay. I was *not* gay.

Not gay, not gay, not gay, not gay.

I squeezed my eyes shut and repeated the words over and over again in my mind, as if they were a mantra. But somehow, no matter how hard I tried, he found his way back to the forefront of my mind again. Jordan freaking Hughes.

Why did he kiss me? Did he think I was gay? Because I was pretty sure I mentioned more than once that I wasn't. Not that I'd ever really been in a relationship with a girl before, or anyone for that matter. I just knew I wasn't gay. I couldn't be. I'd never thought about a guy like that before. It felt wrong. That wasn't who I was. That may have been who Jordan was, but not me.

I was not—

"Honey! Am I ordering a pizza tonight?" My mother's voice interrupted my thoughts. I quickly blinked away the moisture in my eyes, turned on my side to face the wall, and feigned sleep. I didn't want to deal with anyone right now. I wanted to just lay there forever, untouched and undisturbed.

"Elliot? Are you home?" I could hear my mother's

footsteps as she ascended the stairs. Before long, the door to my bedroom creaked open, letting a pool of light from the hallway flood into my dark room.

"Eli?" she whispered as she poked her head in. She must have seen the lump on the bed, because a few seconds later, the mattress dipped as she sat beside me. She was quiet for a while before I felt her hand reach out and gently touch the bruising around my nose. I winced away from her but pretended to still be asleep. "Sorry," she whispered. I was thankful that we had already had a discussion about bullying years ago, so she knew where I stood and how I wanted to deal with situations like this. Basically, I had drawn a line and had told her not to cross it. I told her that I was more comfortable dealing with it on my own and that if I ever couldn't handle it, then I would invite her past that boundary. I knew it killed her, but it was what I wanted, and she did her best to respect that.

She placed her hand gently on my upper arm, rubbing her thumb over my shoulder. "I know you're trying to be strong, honey," she said softly. "But it's okay to ask for help." I heard her exhale at my lack of a response. After a few more moments of silence, she leaned down and placed a soft kiss on my cheek. "I love you."

And then she left me in peace. I didn't have the heart to open my eyes again. I simply drifted off to sleep with thoughts of blue-green eyes and a crooked smile.

Ø

I woke up to morning light shining in through my window.

I squinted against it before checking the time on my smartphone: 10:21 a.m. It jumped out at me in large font as soon as I pressed the power button. I immediately panicked—I was supposed to have been at school two and a half hours ago.

I flew out of bed and rushed to my door, wincing at the pain coursing through my body. I had to slow down as I made my way downstairs.

The house was empty, that much I could tell. In the kitchen, I found a piece of paper stuck to the fridge. I walked over to it and slipped it out from under the magnet. It was a note from Mom.

Eli,
I called you in sick today. You looked like you needed a day off.

Make sure to keep icing that bruise. Your leftovers from last night are in the fridge.

Your father and I won't be home until late. Don't burn the house down.
—Mom

I sighed and dropped the note on the counter, then pulled another ice pack out of the freezer. I pressed it against my face and took a seat at the kitchen island. At least I wouldn't have to deal with Morgan, Nate, and Cole today. Or Jordan.

Mostly Jordan.

His name triggered the cycle of thought all over again. I felt so confused. Why had he kissed me? Everything was so messed up. It would all be different now because of that one little action.

Had it always been like this? Had he been gay this entire time and I was just stupid enough not to notice? I nearly fell off my stool when I recalled some of the things he had said to me over the course of our short friendship. Now that I knew he was gay—and interested enough in me to actually act on it—they all took on a whole new meaning.

I'll drip if you swirl.

"Oh God, oh God, oh God, oh God," I said in one long breath as I buried my fingers in my hair.

It's not like you're unattractive or anything.

I breathed heavier as panic started to set in. How had this happened? How had I *let* this happen? How had I not *seen* it? My thoughts wandered back to the kiss. I found myself evaluating it, dissecting it, and as it replayed in my mind for the millionth time, I felt my chest constrict, my cheeks reddening even more.

The funny feeling was back.

Making an odd and uncomfortable noise as I moved, I slid off my stool and filled a glass of water, which I downed quickly before tossing the ice pack back in the freezer. I wasn't hungry—I had too much on my mind to be hungry—so I went back upstairs to my room and collapsed on my bed, pausing only to set the now-warm ice pack from last night on my nightstand before curling back up in my blankets.

My stomach ached where Mason and Nate had punched me, my ribs were sore, and moving normally was hard. Curling up into the only comfortable position I could find, I tried to force myself back to sleep. If my brain was going to continue insisting that I think about Jordan, then I would at least try and sleep in hope there was some chance of forgetting and thinking it was all a dream.

Unfortunately, sleep was particularly elusive at the moment. After tossing and turning for nearly half an hour, I rolled over and grabbed my phone from its spot on my nightstand. I couldn't help but feel disappointed at the lack of messages—I would've figured Jordan would have at least *tried* to apologize. I mean, who kisses a guy and then just walks away like nothing even happened?

I opened up my messages and stared at Jordan's name in my contacts. I thought briefly about texting him, calling him even, but ultimately decided against it. We obviously needed to talk about what happened and get things sorted out. I just needed to be calm and collected so that I could tell him that I wasn't gay. He would understand, wouldn't he? He wouldn't try to kiss me again.

But at even the thought of him kissing me again, I felt that funny feeling in my stomach return along with a fresh blush creeping up in my cheeks.

Groaning, I tossed my phone back on the nightstand and pulled the covers up over my head.

This was not good.

Ø

Later that day, when venturing downstairs for food, the last thing I expected to find was a redhead cocooned in a mountain of blankets on our couch. She had the television on, though it was playing commercials at the moment, and was munching on a bowl of cheddar-flavored popcorn.

"What are you doing here?" I asked Holiday tiredly, though the last thing I thought I should be after so much sleep was tired. Her hawklike gaze swiveled over at the sound of my voice. Her thick black eyeliner really made her green eyes pop, even in the dim light from the single side-table lamp on in the room.

"Marathoning *The Bachelorette* with your sister," she said, gesturing at the television screen as if it should have been obvious. I watched the commercial that was on, advertising some anti-aging cream, and looked back at her. I guess that explained why we had a whole new season of the show taped on our DVR. I had honestly thought my mother was responsible, but now I could see my sister was the true culprit. She and Holiday must have been planning this for a while.

"You don't seem like the type of person who would enjoy a dating show," I told her honestly.

"Oh, I'm here to make fun of the process," she assured me, tossing a piece of popcorn high up into the air before catching it almost effortlessly in her mouth.

I nodded. That sounded more like her.

"You coming back to school tomorrow? Jordan seemed pretty distressed when you didn't show up today."

"Did he?" I asked. The thought of him already had me spiraling again.

Holiday simply shrugged noncommittally.

"You feeling okay, Elliot?" I turned at the sound of my sister's worried voice as she entered the room behind me carrying her own bowl of popcorn—regular microwave, as opposed to the cheddar stuff Holiday was eating, which you had to buy in a bag. I noticed her staring at my nose. I hadn't looked in the mirror yet. I hoped it wasn't too bad.

"I came down to get some food." I smiled weakly as she nestled into the couch beside Holly, who had somehow found the remote in her sea of blankets and was now fast-forwarding through the rest of the commercials since my sister had returned.

"There's still some pizza in the fridge from last night," she said. "Oh, and Mom and Dad went out for a date night tonight. They probably won't be home until around ten."

I nodded, already moving toward the kitchen.

"I didn't miss anything, did I?" I overheard Ellie asking Holiday as I left the room. "Is that Ryan Reynolds-looking guy still on, or did she send him home after their date?"

Their conversation drifted away as I made my way into the kitchen. Standing in front of the open refrigerator door to review my options, it was pretty obvious that pizza was my best one, so I stooped down to where the box was nestled into the lower shelf. It was crooked. Whoever had put it in the fridge last had just balanced it on top of all of the other items that were already in there instead of trying to make room for it.

Too lazy to actually take the pizza box out of the fridge so I could open it properly, I lifted the lid just enough to shove my hand in and pull out two pieces of cold meat lovers pizza. Not even bothering with a plate, I closed the refrigerator door and turned and headed back up to my room.

Ellie stopped me again while I was walking through the

living room. "You're welcome to stay down here and watch with us if you'd like," she told me.

On any other day, I might've said yes, but I just wasn't feeling up to it at the moment. In a small voice, I said, "No, thank you."

One side of El's lips drew to the side, as if she was unsure if she wanted to smile at me or frown. I kept my head down and carried my cold pizza back upstairs so I could sulk in peace.

HOW DO YOU KNOW?

"Elliot."

I woke the next day to the soft sound of my sister's voice. My mom must have called me in sick again, because according to my phone, it was already around six thirty Wednesday night. My muscles ached from being in bed for too long, but I still didn't have any desire to leave it. Though in my defense, I had been awake until about four in the morning, mostly because I couldn't stop thinking about Jordan.

I mumbled an incoherent jumble of words in hopes that she would leave me alone, but she sat on the edge of my bed, and a moment later, the scent of fresh pasta reached my nose. An embarrassingly loud gurgle echoed from my stomach and I suddenly regretted sleeping all day.

"Elliot. You need to eat something," Ellie said, as if reading my mind. She gently shook my shoulder.

I groaned and peeled my eyes open. I looked up; her lips were pursed.

"Eat," she commanded, thrusting a bowl of spaghetti into my hands. I looked at her skeptically, and she added, "Don't worry. I cooked it, not Mom."

I sat up, grabbed the fork from her, and did as she told me to.

"Talk to me."

"What?" I asked.

"Something's happened," she said plainly. "You haven't been eating, and you've barely left this room in two days. Not to mention, there's a giant bruise on your face. What's going on?"

"Nothing," I mumbled, staring down at the steaming bowl in my hands. I took comfort in its warmth.

"I'm not stupid, Eli. Tell me," she said firmly.

Staring into her coppery-brown eyes, so much like my own, I finally felt my emotions coming back to me. There was a twisting sensation in my stomach—I felt my heart rise and my throat close over. Tears stung as they gathered in my eyes. I looked down quickly, afraid she'd see my tears, and focused on keeping my breathing even—easier said than done.

"Eli," she said again, somehow enacting a motherly tone.

I hated when she did that. It made it impossible for me to hide things from her, and she knew exactly what she was doing.

"They beat me up," I told her.

"Morgan and Nate?"

I nodded.

"What was it about this time?" she asked softly.

"They were saying some nasty stuff about my friend and me. I don't know. I guess I just snapped. I punched Nate in the face. They returned the favor and then some."

"That's not all that happened," she said knowingly.

I hesitated. "How can you tell?" I asked weakly.

Ellie gave me a small smile. "You're my brother, Eli. I can tell you're upset about something. Something more than the bruises, I mean."

I met her eyes again, and the emotions I'd been trying to keep in check bubbled up in my throat. It was overwhelming—I couldn't stop myself from saying what I said next. "He kissed me." I choked out the words at barely a whisper, a single tear rolling down my cheek.

She heard it anyway, and in a calm, nonjudgmental tone, asked, "Who?"

"Jordan." His name was the key that unlocked the rest of my tears. Several spilled out without permission, and I hurriedly swiped them away with the back of my hand.

"Okay. . . . Well, did you like it?" she asked softly.

"I'm not gay," I said quickly, my voice wavering slightly.

"That wasn't what I asked."

"I'm not gay," I repeated, quieter this time.

"How do you know?"

"What?" I looked up at her, surprised.

"How do you know that you're not gay?"

"I don—"

"Have you ever been with a guy before?" she asked simply.

"What? No," I said, confused at where this conversation was going.

"Have you ever been with a girl before?"

"No," I mumbled, my embarrassment growing by the second.

"Ever given either one a remote chance?"

"Not really," I said softly.

"Then how do you know?"

I didn't answer. I didn't know how to.

"People are complicated, Eli," she explained calmly after an awkward silence. "It's hard to figure out how other people work, but sometimes it's even harder to understand ourselves. Take me for example. It took a long time for me to figure this out, but I identify as asexual. And aromantic, if we're being technical."

"What do you mean?" I asked. I'd never heard the terms before.

She adjusted how she was seated on my bed, folding up her legs to get more comfortable. "It means I don't feel *that way* about guys or girls. It's like the opposite of bisexual. Bisexual people are open to being intimate with members of either gender. People who are asexual aren't interested in being intimate with either, or anyone else for that matter—trans, nonbinary, or intersex. Aromantic is similar in concept but with regard to the romantic aspects of a relationship as opposed to the sexual ones. I've never been interested in being with anyone, and I don't see myself being interested anytime in the future," she said. "That could change at some point—this stuff is all fluid. That's the thing about sexualities: they aren't set in stone. By identifying one way or another, you aren't signing a contract that says this is who you are or have to be for the rest of your life. I identify as asexual now, but there may come a day when I meet somebody and fall in love with them and want to explore my sexuality. And that's okay. Sexualities change as people do. All I know for certain is that this is the way I feel now."

I let that sink in for a few moments. What she was saying made sense. People were dynamic. They were constantly changing. Why should that mean their sexual orientations were any different. Sure, I had assumed I was straight for most of my life, but I hadn't really ever acted on that assumption. Maybe I had been like Ellie in a way. Not completely, but partially maybe. I'd never really had a crush on anyone. But now there was the whole Jordan thing.

"How long have you known you were . . . asexual?" I asked out of curiosity.

"I think I've always kind of known," she said, shrugging. "I just didn't know it had a name until a few years ago."

"So that's why you've never brought home a boyfriend?" I smirked.

"Shut up." She laughed and shoved my shoulder. "What's your excuse?"

"Too busy being beat up."

Her laughter died quickly. "I'm sorry about that," she said, the mood shifting back to solemn. "I know you only stepped in to keep them away from me."

Back in middle school was when I first saw Nate and Morgan turn their attention to her. Ellie was more introverted back then. She only really opened up when Holiday or I was with her. We were in gym class. I had just come out of the boy's locker room and she was still waiting on the bleachers for Holiday. When I spotted her, I saw Nate and Morgan standing over her, but it wasn't until I got closer that I realized what they were saying. They were making fun of her hair, which was thicker and wilder back then, as she hadn't yet figured out the right combination of hair products and flatironing techniques to properly tame it.

They had said she looked ugly. They also said some stuff about her being a teacher's pet or something, and that that was the only reason she got such good grades. She ignored them, and instead focused more on her fingernails than what they were saying. She put on a blank face, but having lived with her my whole life, I knew how to see beyond that. I knew their words were getting to her, so I hadn't thought twice before I stepped between them. I was never a very social kid, so I didn't really have any friends at that point. Sure, I knew everybody, and nobody seemed to have any problems with me, but I still chose to hang around my sister and her friend because I wasn't close to anyone else. I think that was part of the reason I hadn't minded getting involved. I had nothing to lose by standing up to them, and I'd have rather seen my sister happy than being picked on by a couple of assholes like them.

"You're my sister. It's my job to protect you."

"You never should've needed to." She sighed. "It's all my fault."

"What do you mean? Just because you're smarter than them doesn't mean it's your fault they started bullying you."

"They never bullied me because I was smart, Eli," she said.

"What?"

"Nate used to have a huge crush on me," she said, much to my surprise. "He tried to get me to go out with him, but I rejected him outright because I wasn't interested in being in a relationship with anyone. He didn't take that well. And Morgan doesn't have a good home life. I think his dad is an alcoholic and pretty abusive, so all he can do to get some semblance of control in his life is to make other people feel small. When I rejected Nate, Morgan was all too eager to jump on board to get revenge on me. That's when they both started teasing me."

"I never knew that," I said.

"It's not something that they go around advertising. I only know about Morgan because Holly found some police reports listed in the newspaper a while back and told me about them. I don't know what Cole's story is—he started at school after I left, but I'm sure he has his own reasons for bullying too. I'm not saying that it's justified or anything, I just—I don't know. I feel sorry for them in a way." She regarded me. "Though it's significantly harder to feel bad for them after seeing what they've done to you."

I brought my hand up and lightly touched my injured nose.

"I know it doesn't make much of a difference now," she continued, "but I don't think I ever thanked you for protecting me like you did. I'm only sorry that you had to."

"It's fine," I assured her, poking at my bowl of spaghetti. "What do I do about Jordan?"

"Well . . . did you feel anything when he kissed you?" she asked.

I shrugged. "I don't know. There was a weird feeling in my stomach, I guess."

"A good feeling or a bad feeling?"

"I can't tell."

Ellie sighed. "I don't know if I'll ever fall in love with anybody. I don't even know if I can feel love. Romantic love, anyway. I know I love you, and Mom and Dad, but that's different. Love . . . falling in love is a strange concept for me, but I do know that it is beautiful and precious. If someone can make you feel that way, it shouldn't matter what gender they are. I can't pretend to know what you are feeling right now, but if there's any inkling of a possibility that you might like him, too, then I think you should chance it. We won't love you less, no matter what you decide."

"Really?"

"Yeah. Maybe you're gay. Maybe you're not. You could be bi, or demi, or a million other things that not even I know about. Hell, maybe you're just Jordansexual. I don't know the answer. You might not know for a long time, either, and that's okay. All that matters is that you are *you*, and you will always be my exceptionally dull little brother." She grinned.

"We're four minutes apart," I protested. "And just because you're some supernerd doesn't mean I'm stupid. I'll have you know I'm doing well in all my classes."

"Yes, because it's so hard to ace gym." She rolled her eyes.

"Shut up," I whined.

She got up off my bed. "Just think about what I said,

Eli. You might surprise yourself." With that, she left my room, closing the door behind her. I stared down at the partially eaten bowl of spaghetti in my hands and thought about two things: if the kiss made me feel *that way* about Jordan, and how the hell my sister knew literally everything.

Ø

I felt awkward as all hell walking into school the next day, even more so than usual. It was a Thursday now, and I'd been gone since the incident on Monday. I feared that everyone would somehow know what had happened between me and Jordan. Like they'd stare and point and lash out at me for something I hadn't even done.

So I kept my head down and avoided eye contact with any and all people. Maybe if I didn't look at them, they wouldn't be able to peer into my soul and reveal to all the moment that played on repeat in my memories. Instead of going straight to my locker, though, like I normally did, I took a detour and went to the nurse's office.

Lisa looked up from her desk and frowned at me as soon as I entered her office. "Are you hurt already, Mr. Goldman?"

"This happened the other day," I said, gesturing to the purplish bruises around my nose and under both eyes. It was starting to look like I hadn't been sleeping, though the opposite was true. I had borrowed some of Ellie's founda- tion to try and cover the marks up as best I could, but the coverage wasn't as full as I'd hoped, and the darkest areas were still visible. "I've been home for the past couple of days recovering from a broken nose. It still hurts pretty bad, though, and I was wondering if I could be exempt from PE for today."

"A broken nose? Good Lord, how did you manage that? Did somebody hurt you?" She lifted both of her brows at me in astonishment, coming closer and analyzing my nose.

"I got mugged on my way home," I lied. I would deal with the true culprits at some other point—when the time was right.

I thought about what Ellie had said. Despite every instinct in my body telling me not to, I did feel a bit of sympathy for Morgan and Nate, though not enough to forgive them. I wasn't as bitter about Cole, since he hadn't hit me and kind of stood up for me the other day by getting the other two to back down. I still wasn't sure if that was meant to be for my benefit or theirs, but it was enough for me to not reveal to the nurse that they were responsible for my injuries—at least not until I figured out what I wanted to do about it.

"Oh dear, should I call the police?" she asked, concerned.

I shook my head. "It's been dealt with already."

"Good. I don't like the thought of some crazy person out there mugging people. Do you know who it was?"

"No." I shook my head again for emphasis.

"Hm," she hummed, seeming to think on it. "Well, regardless, I'm glad you made it back safely."

"Me too," I said, feeling more awkward than usual.

She smiled weakly and wrote out my exemption slip.

The bell rang for first period. After thanking her, I folded the note, placed it in the pocket of my hoodie, and headed off to class.

BACK FROM THE DEAD

I skipped lunch. I probably could've used something to eat, but I really didn't want to deal with everyone just yet. Instead, I found myself outside of Mrs. Reed's classroom. Steeling myself, I took a deep breath and walked in.

"Elliot," she said, a bit surprised as she looked up from her small lunch of mostly fruit and assorted nuts. "How are you?"

"I've been better." I sighed. "Can I sit in here for lunch period?"

"Of course," she said, gesturing to the many empty desks. Grateful, I walked over to one and dropped my backpack beside it before sliding into the seat.

She eyed me up and down, a mix of suspicion and concern in her eyes. "I sense something is troubling you," she said after a few minutes of silence, though I could tell she wanted to say more. I looked up at her and shrugged noncommittally. "This may not help you," she said, continuing, "but whenever something is bothering me, I try to write stuff down. It doesn't have to be about what's bothering you. It can be about anything, really. Sometimes it's best to write about the things that aren't bothering you to help get your mind off the things that are. Or it can be about things you're trying to figure out or accomplish. It helps me to wrap my head around things, even if all I do is crumple it up and throw it away when I'm finished."

"I might try that," I said. At this point, I was willing to try anything that might help me make sense of the chaos storming around in my brain.

I reached into my backpack and pulled out a notebook and a mechanical pencil. I opened the notebook up to a fresh page and stared at the blank lines. What could I write about?

My name is Elliot Goldman.

That was a start, I guess. I tapped the pencil eraser against the page a few times before continuing to write.

I was born almost eighteen years ago on a cold December day, four minutes and thirteen seconds after my twin sister, Ellie Goldman. We were both named after our great-grandmother Eleanor, though she passed away shortly before we were born.

Ellie and I were very close growing up. We were practically inseparable, but that started to change around the time we entered middle school. Ellie is really smart. I'm not. And so I kind of got left behind.

I took a deep breath, unsure if I wanted to continue writing. I glanced at the clock and decided to continue.

I felt alone during the years that followed, and even though I was never officially diagnosed, I think I fell into a sort of depression. I was sad all the time, tired, and I didn't feel like doing anything.

I exhaled slowly, allowing the words to formulate in my head before I gained the courage to write them down.

That all changed when I met Jordan Hughes.

I shook my head, ripped the page out of the notebook, and crumpled it up as tightly as I could. I couldn't think about that right now. I couldn't think about him. I shoved the small wad of paper into the deepest recess of my backpack and put my head down on the desk. I wished I could go home and curl up in my bed again.

But I couldn't.

Not yet, anyway. I first had to endure the class of doom: AP Chemistry. A full hour of awkwardly sitting next to *him*. A full hour of debating what to say, if anything. A full hour of wishing I was anywhere but there. A full hour of feeling nervous and uncomfortable.

I gave up on sleeping and walked up to Mrs. Reed and told her quietly that I was going to deliver my exemption slip to Mr. Mason. She nodded in return. I went out into the hallway. Thankfully, everyone was still at lunch, so the halls were, for the most part, blissfully empty.

I took my time wandering to Mr. Mason's office, taking great lengths to avoid the cafeteria. Well, the cafeteria and one particular person. Until I figured things out, my plan was to avoid Jordan as much as possible. The less I saw of him, the less chance there was that something would happen between us.

And that's what I wanted . . . right?

Dammit. Why was this so freaking confusing? Why did Jordan have to come into my life? Why wouldn't he leave my head? Why did I sort of want him to kiss me again?

I inhaled sharply and stopped walking, glancing around nervously. I felt paranoid that someone would somehow *know* what I was thinking about. That someone would *know* I was picturing his warm, soft lips and his feathery brown hair—

Dammit.

Not gay. Not gay. Not gay. Not gay.

Not. Gay.

I rounded the corner by Mr. Mason's office and paused upon hearing voices coming from within.

"This school does not tolerate violent behavior, Mr. Hughes."

"I'm sorry, Mr. Mason." I felt my whole body go numb at the sound of his voice. "But I do not tolerate bullies."

"That does not give you the right to physically attack Mr. Decker." Mr. Mason let out a heavy sigh. "Look, Jordan. You're a good kid. I don't want you to mess this up. If you have a problem with any of the students here, please take it up with the people in the office."

"I would love to," Jordan said, unimpressed. "If they would do anything to fix those problems."

"Can you just promise me you won't get into another fight? It's only your first offense, so I'm willing to let you off with a warning."

"Only if you promise not to turn a blind eye next time you see someone being picked on."

"I'll do what I can, Jordan."

"Then, so will I."

Mr. Mason sighed again. "All right. You're dismissed. You might as well head to the gym. Class starts in three minutes."

"Yes, sir."

I heard Jordan get up to leave. I wasn't ready to see

him, not in person, not after what happened. Panicking, I immediately turned and looked for a place to hide.

"Elliot?"

Shit.

I slowly turned to him, and had to gulp down the lump in my throat. "H-Hi," I stuttered.

Smooth, Elliot, smooth.

He looked like he wanted to say something more, but right then, Mr. Mason stepped out of his office. "Ah, Mr. Goldman. Back from the dead I see."

"Ha-ha, yeah," I said awkwardly, fidgeting with my fingers. I reached into my hoodie pocket and pulled out my exemption slip and held it in the air. "I, um, came to give you this."

Mr. Mason took the slip from me, scanned it briefly, and nodded.

"I was wondering if I could spend next period in the library. It's quiet there, and I have quite a bit of homework to catch up on."

"Sure, Eli." He smiled at me before turning to Jordan again. "Coming, Mr. Hughes?"

Jordan looked down at his shoes as he reluctantly followed Mr. Mason. I watched as they made their way toward the gym. At the last moment, Jordan hesitated and glanced back at me. Our eyes met and my heart fluttered all over again. A smirk tugged at the corners of his lips.

I scowled at him before they disappeared around the corner, though I could already feel the fresh blush blooming on my cheeks at being caught staring.

Dear Lord. Kill me now.

COME NOW, ELI

Focus, Elliot, focus!

I kept my gaze fixed stubbornly on the number two pencil held firmly in my white-knuckled grip. I couldn't look away, nor could I tune in to Ms. Dailey's lecture enough to start taking notes. I just sat there with the tip of my pencil pressed against the blank notebook paper as I tried not to hyperventilate.

I didn't know how I expected to make it out of this class without passing out, but whatever plan I'd had was tossed out the window the minute *Jordan freaking Hughes* took his seat beside me.

God, he was right there.

I had yet to turn and look at him, but then I didn't really need to. I could practically feel his presence beside me, like a wave of heat sending goose bumps up my left arm.

A sudden escalation of noise and the rustling of papers meant Ms. Dailey was handing out the homework assignment. I bit my lip, knowing I was screwed for not paying any attention to the lecture. Sighing, I let go of the pencil and waited patiently for my paper to arrive.

I nearly jumped out of my skin when Jordan brushed his knuckles against my forearm to gain my attention. I reluctantly turned to look at him and, seeing the genuine concern in his eyes, immediately regretted it.

"Are you okay? How are you feeling?" he asked. Instead of answering, I looked down at my pencil again to avoid making any sort of eye contact.

Conflicted. Confused. Mortified. Panicked. Anguished. Curious. Freaked the hell out. Shall I go on?

I didn't trust myself to answer, so I didn't.

"Look, I'm sorry," he whispered as our papers came around. "I didn't mean to hurt you."

I nearly broke at the sound of defeat in his voice. I couldn't help but glance at him out of the corner of my eye. I shouldn't have, though, because now I needed to add *guilty* to that list. I knew I needed to say something—anything, really. I opened up my mouth and forced words to come out.

"I-I'm just . . . freaking out," I whispered honestly, keeping my gaze strictly on the pencil.

I could feel his gaze burning a hole through the side of my face, but I refused to turn and look at him. Thankfully, after a few minutes of excruciating silence, Ms. Dailey approached our desk and gave me the work I'd missed.

"Thanks," I mumbled, finally glancing down at my worksheet on atomic theory.

"Feeling better, Mr. Goldman?" she asked. I nodded

absentmindedly. She glanced between Jordan and me. "I figured Mr. Hughes here could catch you up on what you missed. If you have any questions that he can't answer, then you may ask me."

Isn't that just the cherry on top?

I gave a faint nod and etched my name across the top of the paper. Hopefully I wouldn't need any help at all. That way I could avoid both of them and just turn in my assignments at the end of the week.

Jordan, thankfully, remained silent as she walked away. I wasn't ready to deal with him. Frankly, I wasn't sure I'd ever be ready to deal with him. I was just going to try and ride out the rest of the period without uttering a single word.

Ø

At the sound of the bell, a tsunami of relief washed over me. In the blink of an eye, I scooped up my bag, slung it over my shoulder, and hightailed it out of the room.

I hadn't even made it to my locker before a hand closed around my arm and guided me away. At first I feared it was Morgan, Nate, or Cole, but my stomach flipped when I turned and saw Jordan. He led me out the nearest set of doors and walked me toward the school's baseball diamond. It wasn't baseball season, so nobody would be out there.

A string of curse words started to form in my mind and I immediately wanted to give in to my instincts to run as far away as my feet would carry me. Unfortunately, Jordan's grip on my arm kept me from doing that, so instead, I did my best to force down any signs of panic.

I knew, in the back of my mind, that he wasn't going to hurt me, but my fight or flight instincts were on high alert knowing the two of us would soon be alone. I wasn't ready to be alone with him again. I was still trying to process what had happened the last time we were alone together.

I needed time. I needed space. I needed to think.

But apparently, I wasn't going to get any of that.

It became harder to breathe past the lump forming in my throat. It was that ache behind my windpipe that I had become all too familiar with over the last couple of days. I felt like I was going to burst into tears at any second. Panicked, frustrated, confused tears.

I swallowed several times to try to get the feeling to ease up, but it only seemed to grow as the distance between us and privacy shrunk.

Everything was changing . . . and I wasn't ready for it.

Jordan tugged me inside one of the brick dugouts and brought me closer to the inside wall so we were out of sight of anyone leaving school. He stayed close, though. He held my upper arms, his eyes staring straight into my soul.

I didn't breathe. I couldn't. Everything was spiraling. I wasn't ready. I wasn't ready to confront what had happened. All I wanted right now was to put this whole situation on the back burner and run away from my problems. I didn't want to deal with it. It made my head hurt, and my stomach flip every time I tried to. But Jordan wasn't giving me the option to run away.

"Tell me you felt nothing," he said. I looked at him, perplexed. "Tell me you felt nothing, and I'll leave you alone."

I looked away, rubbing my forearm nervously as I tried to figure out what I wanted to do, because I honestly didn't know. This was all so new and confusing. I felt so torn.

"You just have to say the words, Eli," he breathed, leaning closer, motioning like he was going to kiss me again.

"W-What are you doing?" I stuttered, placing my hands on his chest to keep him where he was.

"Convincing you," he said, softly caressing my cheek with his fingers.

"What?"

"I know what's going through your head, Eli. I've been through it myself." Reluctantly, I looked up and met his gaze—there was only sincerity there. I was unable to look away. He continued speaking. "You're confused. You're scared. Everything you thought you knew has been flipped upside down and sideways, and you can't make sense of any of it. You feel like you've been blindfolded and tossed into frigid water. Now you're struggling to figure out which way is up while trying not to drown."

"Did you rehearse that?" I asked, wondering how else his little speech could've come out so smoothly.

"Maybe?" He gave a nervous smile and then shook his head. "It doesn't matter. It's how you're feeling, isn't it?"

Was it?

Everything I thought I knew felt like it was changing; that part was true. Like my life had a mind of its own and I was simply being dragged behind it as it ran off in its own direction. But drowning? Did I feel like I was drowning?

In a way, I supposed I did. It was hard to breathe when I was around Jordan. That cold, icy panic that seemed to overtake me every time I thought about him? The odd weight in my stomach when I thought about what it all meant? I didn't have control. My world was spiraling, and all I could do was hold on as it fell into chaos. I didn't know which way was up. Maybe I was drowning.

The more his words echoed around in my skull, the more I realized they were true.

"Oh God . . . what's happening to me?"

"You're in denial, Elliot, and I'm going to help fix that," he said with newfound determination. To be honest, it kind of scared me, seeing the resolve in his eyes, yet at the same time, it was exciting.

"Why? Why me?" I asked.

An easy smile spread across his lips. "Oh, come now, Eli." His breath fanned against my skin as he stared down at me. His hands were pressed against the wall on either side of me, preventing my escape. My heart rate accelerated significantly. "You can't deny we have chemistry together."

I narrowed my eyes at his pun. We had chemistry *class* together. We were freaking lab partners. But he didn't mean it that way. His tone insinuated a different kind of chemistry.

He was taller than me, so I straightened my spine and looked him straight in the eye. In a surprisingly steady voice, I said, flat out, "I'm. Not. Gay."

A deep chuckle resonated in his chest. He leaned in close to my ear. My breath caught in my throat once more as his lips brushed the base of my jaw. I didn't move. I couldn't.

"And yet . . ." he whispered before backing away, exiting

the dugout, and disappearing altogether, leaving me standing there alone, confused, and a little flustered.

What had I gotten myself into?

COOKIE DOUGH

Yet.

My breath came out in short, uneven spurts as I walked down the street. I was functioning on autopilot—my brain was too preoccupied to take any responsibility over my body.

W-What are you doing?

Convincing you.

What the hell? What if I didn't want to be convinced? God, this was so messed up. Why couldn't I just get through senior year without talking to anybody but Holly and my family? Why couldn't I just be that one kid who gets picked on every now and then?

Why did I have to be the kid Jordan kissed? Why did I have to be the kid questioning his sexuality?

I'm not gay.

How do you know?

At this point, I would gladly have curled up in a hole and died if it meant not having to face the world. When had my life become so complicated? Actually, I knew exactly when: the moment *Jordan freaking Hughes* waltzed into it.

I glanced around then and realized I was already over halfway home. How had that happened? I shook my head and picked up the pace. I just wanted to get home, where I could be alone and think about my problems without getting run over.

I was home before too long. As soon as I unlocked the front door and walked in, I smelled cookies. More accurately, burning cookies. I rushed into the kitchen and found my mother pulling a pan of blackened chocolate chip cookies out of the oven. She coughed as she set them down atop the stove and waved her oven mitts in the air to try and clear away the smoke.

"What are you doing?" I asked for the second time that day.

"I came home early and was going to make you some cookies to help you feel better, but, well, I'm not a very good cook, am I?" she rambled.

"You should definitely stick to your day job, Mom," I said, chuckling as I approached the oven. The cookies were beyond saving, but I still dipped my finger into the mixing bowl and tasted what was left of the cookie dough. It was salvageable.

"Honey, what's wrong?" Mom asked. I looked up at her as she was moving her hands toward my face. I pulled away, but she continued, touching my cheeks, wiping the moisture from them. Had I been crying? I hadn't even noticed.

"It's nothing," I said quickly, wiping at my face with my sleeve. "I think I can save this cookie dough." Without looking at her, I pulled some flour and vanilla out of the cupboard and set to work, adding in a few spare ingredients and mixing the dough until I was satisfied with the flavor and consistency.

I set the bowl between us and grabbed two spoons from the cutlery drawer, handing one to my mom. I started scooping the dough onto a new cookie sheet. She did the same, and as we filled up the empty space on the pan, I periodically stole excess dough from her largest scoops and added them to some of the smaller ones.

It felt nice to be working side by side with her. We didn't say much, but I didn't mind. Just the simple fact that she was there next to me made me feel the slightest bit better.

Once satisfied, I dropped the temperature of the oven to 350 degrees, stole the oven mitts off the counter, and put the cookie sheet in.

"Did I ever tell you how your dad and I met?" my mother asked, laughing to herself at the memory.

"I don't remember if you did," I said, looking at her expectantly.

"We went to the same college. We even stayed in the same dorms that year—freshman year, I think. I was downstairs in the community kitchenette trying to bake some cookies from one of my grandmother's old recipes—I was feeling down about an exam or something, and her cookies always cheered me up when I was a kid. I ended up nearly setting fire to the place, but your dad smelled the burning cookies and came to help me. He was the only person who did. After we got everything to stop smoking, we opened up some windows to air the place out and ended up just sitting and talking while we ate the rest of the cookie dough."

"That doesn't really surprise me," I said, smiling softly. I glanced over at the blackened cookie sheet in the sink. "What made you fall for him?"

"He was the most caring and considerate person I'd ever met," she said simply. "It also helped that he was pretty easy on the eyes back then, and was one of the first guys who truly showed an interest in me."

I hummed a response, somewhat lost in thought. That sounded eerily familiar.

Silence stretched between us for a few moments before my mother changed the subject. "How's your nose?" she asked.

"It feels fine," I said, even though it was still pretty sore. But I didn't need her worrying about it. "It looks worse than it is."

"What happened?" she asked.

I shook my head. "Nothing too exciting, a basketball to the face in gym. It's my fault. I wasn't paying attention."

The way she glared at me told me she knew I was lying. She thankfully didn't call me out on it, though.

"Well, I hope you know I'm here if you ever want to talk about how . . . *uncoordinated* you seem to have been recently. We all are."

"I know, Mom," I said, sighing as I glanced at the timer on the stove. "I'm going to go catch up on some homework. Take these out when the timer goes off."

"Okay, honey. I love you."

"Love you too," I responded, already heading for the stairs. I went up to my room and collapsed on the bed. The cookies had been a nice distraction, but now I was alone with my thoughts again.

I sat up then, opened my backpack, and pulled out my calculus textbook. Might as well try and get some work done before Jordan took over my mind again. However, after staring at limits of functions for a solid hour, I gave up and closed my book, setting it to the side. I couldn't focus. Not with his blue-green eyes haunting my thoughts. I leaned against the headboard and finally opened up my mind, allowing myself to think about Jordan.

Since I had met him, he had been nothing but kind, sweet, and understanding. From helping me to the nurse's office that first day to taking care of me after I'd been beaten up, he hadn't judged me, hadn't tried to smother me with pity. He was just there—whenever I needed him and even when I didn't. He tried to give me a ride home every day. He sat with me at lunch. He stood up to Cole on my behalf while I was gone.

He treated me like an equal.

I realized then that just because he was gay, just because he'd kissed me, it didn't mean he was a different person. He was still the same kind, sweet, and understanding Jordan Hughes.

Even with all this, with what happened between us, it seemed as though he was only trying to help. I had a hard time believing Jordan would do anything purely for personal gain. Though it was in his interests for me to be gay, I knew he wasn't trying to push me. He wanted to help me figure this all out—for my sake, not his.

Have you ever been with a guy before?

What? No.

Have you ever been with a girl before?

No.

Ever given either one a remote chance?

Not really.

Then how do you know?

I swallowed hard and stared up at my ceiling, blinking back a new wave of tears. Why was this so hard? Why was it so *frustrating*? I let out an exaggerated sigh. Ellie was right: I didn't know. And like it or not, Jordan *did* make me feel something. And that had to mean *something*.

I grabbed my phone and opened up the messaging app, letting my thumb hover over Jordan's contact. Despite feeling nervous, I selected his profile and started typing.

Meet me in the park in one hour.

Immediately after seeing that he had read the text, I threw on a sweater and headed back downstairs. My mother had successfully taken the first batch of cookies out of the oven, and they were currently cooling on a rack. I grabbed one and took a bite out of it, nodding in approval at the taste. After evening out the dough proportions she had already started, I helped her get the second batch in the oven before heading to the door and shrugging on my jacket.

"Where are you heading?" my mother asked curiously.

"I'm meeting a friend," was all I gave her as way of an explanation before exiting my home.

It was time to figure things out.

CONVINCE ME

The park was mostly empty when I arrived. It made sense. The days were getting colder, so most of the people around here were keener on staying inside. I couldn't blame them. It felt like it might start snowing at any moment.

I nervously bounced my knee up and down while sitting on a park bench, waiting for Jordan to arrive. I fidgeted with my hands, hoping that I wouldn't lose my nerve and run back home before we had a chance to discuss things. Honestly, I was feeling a bit nauseated at the thought of seeing him again, but I needed to be strong. He was just a person, after all.

Though it was a bit chilly out, I could feel myself sweating. I debated taking my jacket off to try to cool down, but then spotted him in the distance and quickly decided against it. He wore a maroon jacket, and his tawny brown hair was styled to perfection, like always. Mine looked like a mess compared to his. No matter what I did to it, it always looked too wild and fluffy. I swore it had a mind of its own sometimes.

"Elliot?" Jordan asked, tentatively approaching the bench.

I realized then that I'd been starting to hope he wouldn't come. But here he was, looking as kind and sweet and concerned as ever. I thought I was ready to see him again, but looking at him now, I knew I was still terrified. Of what, though, I couldn't tell.

"I need help with my chemistry homework." I lied as a fresh wave of icy panic overtook me. I couldn't do this. I couldn't even look him in the eye.

"Oh." He sounded disappointed. My chest tightened so much that it hurt. "Well, where is it?" he asked.

Dammit. "Um. I guess I didn't bring it." I blushed, realizing the fault in my lie. I should've thought this through. At the very least, I should've had an escape plan already figured out.

"Oh," he said again, and shoved his hands into his pants pockets. "Do you want me to leave then?"

"*No,*" I squeaked a little too quickly. I cleared my throat and lowered my voice to a normal pitch. "No, just—can you—can we walk? Like, over there? There's a path, I think."

Smooth, Eli.

"Yeah, sure." I could hear the confusion in Jordan's tone. He stared at me, unconvinced. "A walk sounds good."

I stood up quickly, shoved my hands into my jacket pockets, and started walking, knowing he would follow. He appeared beside me a few seconds later, the sleeves of our jackets brushing against each other every so often. I exhaled softly, surprised that I couldn't yet see my breath. Autumn was on its way out; there weren't a lot of leaves left on the trees, and the days were becoming colder and shorter.

Not that I felt all that cold. Not with Jordan beside me.

"I've never been back here," Jordan remarked as we followed a hiking path into the forest. We were completely engulfed by trees in a matter of moments. It was getting dark out, too, and that was reflecting in the deepening shadows around us. The forest made it seem even darker, but for some reason, I felt more at ease in a shadowy forest than I would've felt if we were still out in the open. "You're not taking me out here to murder me, are you?"

"No," I said, giving in to his attempt to start a conversation. It was a safe topic. I could work with a safe topic. "I used to hike back here with my family during the summer, when I was younger."

"It's beautiful." He smiled, sweeping his eyes across the exposed branches and what remained of the autumn leaves. Most were on the ground by now, but a few stubborn ones still clung to the branches.

"Yeah, it is. You should've seen it last month when all the leaves were at peak colors." I glanced around a little as well, imagining all of the brilliant reds, yellows, and oranges that had previously painted the forest. My eyes eventually found their way back to the boy at my side and I blushed, discovering his eyes already trained on me.

He smirked, nudged my shoulder. "You're cute when you blush."

Of course, that only made my cheeks turn a deeper shade of red. I flipped up the collar of my jacket and did my best to hide behind it, using my hands to make sure it didn't fall back down.

"Elliot." Jordan chuckled, gently grabbing my wrists

and pulling them away from my face. He didn't let go once he had lowered them. I inhaled sharply.

"Sorry," I said, though, in truth, I wasn't sure what I was apologizing for. Either way, I couldn't hold his gaze for long—it was simply too intense. Instead, I looked at the collar of his shirt again. It was navy blue, a nice shade that brought out the color in his eyes. It looked like a soft material, too, and I found myself wanting to reach out and touch it.

"Why are we out here, Elliot?" Jordan asked.

His question snapped me from my trance. I immediately stumbled over what to say. "I—well—I don't—I want to—I wanted to say that, well—"

"Eli." He chuckled again and brought his fingers to rest under my chin. He gently tilted my head up so that I couldn't look anywhere but at him. "Just take a deep breath and tell me."

I stopped stuttering and just stared into his eyes. They were so vibrant and full of life. I wished I had eyes like his. Mine just looked like dull, faded copper with black dots in the center, almost like someone had drawn a circle in the middle of a penny with a permanent marker.

Looking into those eyes, I made my decision. In a voice so soft I wasn't sure he could hear, I breathed out two words that changed everything: "Convince me." As the words left my lips, a horrible feeling settled in my stomach. I felt awkward and vulnerable. I was starting to worry that I'd said the wrong thing. What if he didn't like me anymore? Maybe I was just being stupid.

But staring at him then, he wore an easy smile. My

breath caught as he took a step closer and gingerly reached out with both hands, placing them on my waist.

I didn't know what to do. I let him take control. Jordan pulled me closer and gently leaned over and pressed his lips to my own. My eyes fluttered closed and my stomach trembled with . . . whatever that feeling was. One of Jordan's hands moved up my side and he tucked a stray tuft of my hair behind my ear, then gently caressed my cheek.

I wanted to cry from the conflicting emotions that were traveling through me all at once. My head was telling me that everything was wrong, but my heart was filled with so much warmth that it felt close to bursting. I was thinking too much. I needed to stop thinking. I did my best to rid the doubts from my mind and tried to focus solely on him.

His lips molded themselves against mine perfectly; there was a certain gentleness as he nipped and tugged at my bottom lip. I realized that I actually kind of liked that he was a little taller than me. It somehow felt more natural than the thought of kissing someone shorter. It felt better.

I think I surprised us both when I buried my fingers in his feather-soft hair and tentatively started to kiss him back. Somewhere in the back of my mind I knew I should've been embarrassed by my obvious inexperience, but at that moment I didn't care. I couldn't think about anything but the boy in front of me.

His tongue traced my bottom lip, but it wasn't until he lightly pinched my ass and pulled me even closer that I realized he wanted me to open my mouth more. Either way, the startled gasp I made did the trick. Jordan used his tongue to explore the inside of my mouth. It was a weird, foreign experience, but it also felt . . . good.

A soft groan bubbled up my throat without permission and slipped past my lips. I blushed at the noise I'd made.

I clenched my fist in the soft fabric of his shirt. He pulled away from me and started kissing down my cheek, jaw, neck. I greedily inhaled the chilled air, only then realizing how little I'd been breathing. My eyes were still closed, and my skin tingled all over each time his lips moved.

At two spots he made my toes curl with just his lips: just under my ear, and where my neck met my shoulder. He gave both plenty of attention. I was panting so hard, it was as though I'd run a marathon. As he worked his way back up my neck, planting one last kiss on my lips, I knew he felt the same.

Resting his forehead against mine, breathing heavily, Jordan asked, "How'd I do?"

I could only utter one word in response.

"Fuck."

NOT YET

At lunch the next day, I found myself sitting across from Holly again. Of all the people at school, besides Jordan, I felt like she was the only one who wouldn't turn me away or judge me. She was busy working on something on her laptop again, like she always was. I wondered what it was this time.

"What are you up to?" I asked, eyeing the back of her laptop.

She glanced up at me briefly before returning her eyes to her screen. "I'm writing an essay about that short story 'The Most Dangerous Game' for English comp."

"Oh, I think I read that last year." I looked up, trying to remember anything I could about the story. "That's the one about hunters, right?"

"Yeah," she said. "It's about the moral ambiguity of hunting. It explores this by portraying it in an exaggerated sense."

"With the guy who's hunting humans . . ."

"Exactly. General Zaroff is made out to be the bad guy in the story. He's hunting humans, which, naturally, is something that we all believe to be wrong and evil. However, if you look past the hunting humans part, he displays no characteristics of a villain. He is civilized in conversation, passionate about his hobbies, honest about everything when he talks with Rainsford—he even gives the guy genuine advice on how to survive longer on the island. Upon first instinct, everyone wants to think of General Z as this evil, inhuman character, but in reality, the only notable difference between him and normal hunters is the creatures that they hunt. The whole point that Richard Connell is trying to make is that if we think it's morally wrong to hunt a human, then why are we okay with hunting deer, or bear, or . . . I don't know, jaguars?"

"I hope you wrote all of that down," I said. "Your analysis is impressive."

I had never looked that far into it and had simply viewed it as that story with the guy who hunts humans.

"I'm working on it," she said. "I have to find some more sources to back up my theories, though."

"It's going to be a really good essay," I told her with complete confidence.

"Thanks," she said, and she started typing furiously again.

I let her be and looked down at my chosen assortment of barely edible food for the day: cardboard pizza, canned corn, baby carrots, half of a tuna sandwich, and a carton of chocolate milk. I took a bite out of the tuna sandwich to start. Moments later, Jordan sat down beside me. Holiday looked up from her laptop again, throwing curious glances between the two of us before casually asking, "So did you two finally kiss and make up?" I blushed and looked away at her choice of words; thankfully, though, she was already looking back down at her computer screen.

"Yeah, we're all good now," Jordan confirmed.

"That's good," she said, still typing. "I was beginning to worry that I might have to kill you." Jordan's eyes widened. Holly smirked. "I'm just messing with you," she teased.

"Phew," Jordan said, dramatically wiping fake sweat off of his forehead.

I smiled to myself, poking around at the soggy sweet corn on my tray.

"How does a girl like you end up getting a name like Holiday?" Jordan asked after the silence had stretched too long.

"Have you ever heard of a band called Green Day?" she asked.

"Wait," Jordan said, his eyes widening. "Are you named after the song 'Holiday'?"

Holly lifted up the short sleeve of her black Nirvana T-shirt to reveal a tattoo of the heart-shaped grenade symbol from Green Day's *American Idiot* album cover.

"Are you serious?" Jordan asked way too excitedly.

Holly made eye contact with me then and we burst out laughing. "You're so gullible!" She laughed, poking at the corner of her eyes to try to catch the moisture without messing up her eyeliner. "That song came out in 2004. Do I look that young to you?"

"Dang." Jordan deflated, disappointed. "That would've been so awesome."

"I mean it's not that far-fetched either," I said, trying to defend Jordan. "Both of your parents are hard-core punk rockers. It sounds like something they would do."

"That's fair," Holly said, nodding. She looked at Jordan. "The real story is that my parents were really poor at the time, and had finally saved up enough money to go on vacation when they found out my mother was pregnant with me. They had to spend their vacation money preparing to have a child instead of going to Europe, so instead of getting a holiday, they got me."

"Wow," Jordan said, still impressed. "When did you get your tattoo?"

"When I turned sixteen. My parents were pretty chill about it. Especially because I chose something that represented an epic album by an epic band that also had a meaningful connection to me."

"I think you're the most badass person I've ever met," he said. He looked like a kid in a candy shop as she showed him the tattoo again. To be honest, it was kind of cute.

Holly snorted. "What? You mean this guy doesn't fit the bill?"

I blushed, realizing she meant me.

Jordan laughed as he swept over me with his eyes. "I don't think *Elliot* and *badass* belong on the same planet, let alone in the same sentence."

I glared at him with my best attempt at re-creating a Holly-level glare. It was pitiful, and I knew it, but his next words made me blush even harder.

"You're too adorable to be badass."

"Shut up," I muttered, turning so red that if I stood

at an intersection, oncoming cars would think I was a stop sign.

"Aw, don't be embarrassed. You get to be in the same category as puppies, babies, and cats on the internet," Holly cooed.

"I will murder you both. While you sleep. With a spork," I threatened, my arms crossed defiantly.

"I'm sure you will, Eli," Jordan said, laughing.

"I know where you live," I whispered.

He simply laughed again. "Like I said: adorable."

Holly's eyes flitted back and forth between us. For once, she seemed more intrigued with the people actually sitting in front of her than whatever she had going on her laptop. Judging by the look on her face, I could tell the gears in her head were turning about something, but I didn't have a chance to think on it further when I registered Jordan's words.

I narrowed my eyes even farther at him and said the first thing that ambled into my brain: "You know, I'd call you a badass, but there's nothing bad about you—you're just an ass."

What the hell was that, Eli?

Jordan blinked, looking kind of confused. It was almost a compliment, but also kind of an insult at the same time.

"Burn? I think?" Holly said with uncertainty.

"I definitely need to work on my comeback skills," I muttered. They were usually better, but I was having an awful time making my brain work when Jordan was around.

Jordan cleared his throat. "Anyway," he said, turning to me. "Did you want me to help you with some chemistry after school?"

I swallowed, my mind jumping to things that *weren't* chemistry homework. "Sure, that sounds . . . good," I stammered, eyes glued to my tray, thinking *Don't make eye contact, don't make eye contact.*

Expecting him to say something else, it surprised me when he stayed quiet. Instantly, something wet splashed against my arm, and I jumped, surprised to see a carton of milk raining down on Jordan's head. Behind him stood a smug-looking, black-eyed Cole Decker.

"You better think twice before you mess with me again, Hughes," Cole grumbled before walking away.

Jordan growled as he wiped milk off of his face and shook it out of his hair. He looked tense, like he was about to stand up and go after him, but I quickly grabbed hold of his upper arm to keep him in place.

"Bastard," he muttered under his breath, though my touch seemed to soothe him enough to keep him in his seat.

"It's okay, Jordan," I said softly. "He's not worth it."

Holly watched the exchange between us with curiosity. "Hold on—*are* you guys dating?" she asked.

A blush lit my face in neon and I immediately let go of Jordan's arm, electing instead to stare down at my hands, which I folded in my lap. I knew Holly wouldn't care; she was free spirited by nature, but I was still kind of freaked out about the whole *gay* thing.

"No," Jordan said beside me. He shot me a quick glance and a smirk—I could practically hear him mentally adding *not yet* to the end of that sentence.

"Well, you should," she said nonchalantly. "You two would be a hella-cute couple."

M. MONTGOMERY

"*Holly,*" I groaned as the tint of my cheeks darkened. Why were they so intent on teasing me today?

Jordan chuckled. "Well, as much as I'm enjoying this conversation," he said, looking down at his partially soggy shirt, "I think I'm going to go change before class starts."

"Have fun!" Holly grinned at him as he stood up and grabbed his tray. "And don't beat anyone up without telling me first. I want to watch."

"Will do," Jordan agreed, and then made his way out of the cafeteria.

STUDY DATE

"Let's go to my house," Jordan said as I slid apprehensively into the passenger seat of his car. "My mom really wants to meet you."

"What?" I asked, feeling slightly mortified at the prospect of meeting his family.

Jordan bashfully rubbed the back of his neck. "I kind of talk about you a lot."

"Me?"

"Yes, you, silly. Who else would I talk about?"

"I don't know," I replied. "*Anyone* else."

"But what if I don't want to talk about anyone else?" Jordan said.

My eyes were drawn to his pouty lips, and the longer I stared at them, the harder my heart beat in my chest. I pulled my gaze away from him and, peering out at the road ahead, asked the most prominent question that popped into my mind. "Do they . . . know?"

"Know what? That I'm gay?" He chuckled softly.

There it was. The dreaded *g* word. I slowly nodded.

"Yes, they know, and they fully accept it."

"And do they know I'm . . . undecided?"

"That doesn't matter much," Jordan smirked.

"What? Why not?" I asked.

"Because you won't be for long," he said with utter certainty.

"Oh," I stammered. I glanced down at my hands to try to hide my blush. What was this boy doing to me? I couldn't recall ever blushing or stammering this much in my whole life.

"We're here," he said suddenly.

Looking up, I realized we'd pulled into the driveway of a two-story house with faded white siding and a few missing shingles. The garden needed a little upkeep, and the yard needed to be mowed, but other than that, it was nice. Homey.

"Come on," Jordan said, grinning as he opened up his car door. Reluctantly, I did the same. He led me up the steps to the front door and opened it without hesitation. It wasn't locked, so he didn't even need to use a key.

Inside, I was hit by a wall of warmth, the smell of freshly baked bread, and the sounds of utter chaos.

"Layla! Come back here!" It was a voice similar to Jordan's, followed by a squeal. A few seconds later, a little girl came running through the hall to my left wearing nothing but a diaper. She ran straight toward me and clutched my legs tightly as she hid behind me.

I looked down at her with a raised brow, but Jordan only laughed and stooped down to pick her up. She squealed again as her brother lifted her onto his hip and nuzzled her nose with his.

"No. Jordy, no!" she squealed some more, wiggling around in an attempt to escape his arms. "Down!" She kept repeating the command until a younger, shorter, skinnier version of Jordan came around the corner holding a little pink dress in his hands.

"There you are!" he called, causing Layla to squeal and bury her face in Jordan's chest.

It was an adorable sight to see.

Quickly, and with practiced efficiency, Jordan's brother slipped the dress over Layla's head and buttoned the back of it. After that, Jordan set the girl down, and she ran off to some other part of the house.

"Sorry about that," the brother said, sighing before looking at me and smiling. He stuck out his hand in greeting. "I don't think we've met. I'm Drew."

"Elliot," I said, taking his hand in a quick handshake.

"Oh." Drew grinned knowingly and looked at his brother. "I see now."

I blushed again. Looking up, I saw that Jordan was reddening too.

"Shut up, Drew. Where's Mom?"

"In the kitchen," he said before disappearing after his sister.

Jordan shook his head and led me through a living room and dining room on the way back to the kitchen. There, Jordan's mother, a small woman with hair a few shades lighter than Jordan's, stood with her back to us.

"Mom . . . this is Elliot."

Jordan's mother turned around, an excited grin on her face. Right away I could see where he got his smile from. She took a few steps forward and engulfed me in a very tight, very unexpected hug.

"Oh, it's so nice to finally meet you!" she exclaimed. "You're so much more handsome than I imagined."

How much had he been talking about me? Obviously enough to give his mom a description of what I looked like, because as far as I knew, he didn't have any pictures of me for her to compare to. Shaking it off, I sent a pleading look Jordan's way as I gradually lost my ability to inhale.

"Mom. Stop smothering him." Jordan laughed as he tried to pry her off of me. "He's just here to study." Eventually, she did let go, but she kept a hold of my arms so she could look at me properly.

"Well," she said, "my name is Carrie. Feel free to use it."

"Okay," I said, feeling somewhat uncomfortable even as she beamed up at me.

"Will you be staying for dinner?" she asked hopefully.

"Sure, please. I mean, I'm sure my parents won't mind."

"Excellent."

"Okay," Jordan said, cutting in and grabbing my arm. "We're going to go study now."

"Have fun!" she called after us and then returned to what she was doing. Before we reached the stairs she quickly added, "But not too much fun—there are children in this house!"

Tomato. I was the exact shade of one of the tomatoes

I saw sitting on the counter. Jordan, thankfully, didn't say anything as he led me to his room.

His room.

Oh God.

"Make yourself at home," he said as he closed the door and not so subtly locked it. I gulped inaudibly. "I'm going to take a quick shower. I feel like there's still milk in my hair."

"Okay," I said while sliding off my backpack and dropping it at the foot of his bed. Jordan's room had a connected bathroom, which, from the brief glance I got of the interior, looked like it was also accessible from the next room over. Once he'd disappeared inside, I looked around.

My eyes were immediately drawn to a corkboard on the same wall as the door we'd entered through. I walked over to it, noting a bunch of medals and pictures hanging from it. A few of the medals were from Science Olympiad—no surprise there—but others were from athletic competitions. Most of them, and quite a few of the trophies sitting on the far shelf, were from soccer.

I looked at one of the pictures of him nearly horizontal with the ground as he kicked a soccer ball past his opponent. He looked happy and wild at the same time. Other pictures showed him and his Science Olympiad team. I smiled as I found one of him and some short blond girl in lab coats making crazy faces with the world's ugliest lab goggles pressed to their faces. There was also a picture of him with a smaller boy with glasses at what looked like a school pep assembly, or something similar. I wondered who he was.

The bathroom door opened—and I nearly choked on my own saliva when I saw Jordan in a pair of jeans.

And I mean *only* jeans. Turned out he had abs.

"See something you like?" Jordan caught me staring and smirked.

I stared at my battered Converse and didn't answer. I knew that if I tried, I'd be a stuttering mess. My breath caught in my throat as he approached, and soon I was looking at his feet instead of mine. Slowly, I raised my head and was staring once more at his bare chest.

"Eli," he said, looking down at me. "If you want something, you only need to ask."

Ask? Ask what? What did I want?

"I—"

Jordan reached down and gently grabbed my hands. "What do you want, Elliot?"

What *did* I want?

He pulled my hands toward him, lightly guiding my fingertips up his abs, chest, around his neck. He left them there and moved his own hands back down to my waist. "What do you want?" he asked again, staring straight into my eyes.

My heart beat uncontrollably as we stood like that, mere inches from each other.

"Do you want to study?" he asked softly, never breaking our connection. With his fingers he drew light, distracting circles up and down my sides, making it impossible for me to focus properly.

"No," I said, barely a whisper.

"Then tell me, Eli. What do you want?"

In that moment, I listened to my heart instead of my brain. I knew what it wanted. I'd known for a while now. I just didn't want to agree with it. I took a deep breath and looked straight into his eyes. "You."

Jordan obliterated the space between us, pulling me flush against his body. He bent his head and captured my lips with his. I wasn't caught off guard this time and responded immediately, weaving my fingers through his damp hair, tugging slightly. Jordan groaned into my mouth. He squeezed my sides as he pulled me even closer.

This time, I knew what he wanted when he licked my bottom lip. Feeling hesitant but still wanting, I opened my lips for him. Jordan's tongue found its way into my mouth and I nearly forgot how to breathe. His hands slipped under the hem of my shirt and explored my stomach and chest. Suddenly, I felt him grab the hem of the shirt and tug upward.

"Off," he pleaded into me as he tugged the shirt higher and higher. I nodded slightly, and Jordan only pulled away long enough to yank the fabric over my head before slamming our lips together again. He walked us toward the bed. My legs hit the edge and he lowered me down onto the mattress and then hovered over me.

I took the opportunity to trail my fingers back down his chest, tracing every curve and muscle with agonizing slowness. I went lower and lower until he groaned and grabbed my wrists, pinning them to either side of my head.

"Fuck, Elliot," he whispered, looking down at me with his blue-green eyes. This close, I could see that only the outer edges were blue while a ring of green encircled his pupils. "Tell me to stop."

I looked up at him, panting heavily, my lips parted slightly. I didn't know if I wanted him to stop.

"Boys! It's time for dinner!" Jordan's mom called up.

"Fuck," he whispered, still breathing heavily. He was so beautiful, hovering above me, staring directly into my soul. I didn't want to look away. I didn't want to look away ever again.

Shit. I think I'm gay.

DINNER

I was completely zoned out for the first part of dinner. I had too much on my mind to listen to any of the conversations between Jordan's family. It was only when Jordan's mother said my name that I finally turned my attention back to the people around me.

"So, Elliot," Carrie said from across the table as we ate the roasted chicken breast she'd prepared. I looked up at her. "How long have you lived around here?"

"All my life," I told her, sipping from my water glass. "Actually, I grew up about a mile that way"—I pointed west— "but we moved closer to the school when my dad got a promotion at work. I was in middle school at the time."

"And what do your parents do?" She seemed intrigued.

"My dad works for Steinmetz and Happel, and my mother is an engineer."

"Really? What kind is she? Jordan's looking into chemical engineering as a potential career."

"Mechanical," I said before taking a bite of the fresh

bread she'd made earlier that day, along with whatever sauce she'd given us for dipping. "I really like this sauce. It tastes a bit like that garlic butter from Little Caesars but diluted a bit and . . . is that dill?"

Carrie blinked and made eye contact with her eldest son. "Did he really just guess the key to my secret sauce?"

Jordan looked impressed. He shrugged. "Guess so."

"I'm the only one in my family who can cook," I explained. "My parents know how to make a few simple things, but usually, if I don't make dinner, we order in. I've gotten pretty good at experimenting with different flavors and dishes."

"Oh, that's lovely," Carrie said, beaming. "These two can barely make themselves a sandwich without calling for help. Maybe you could teach them a thing or two?"

I caught a glimpse of Jordan looking embarrassed. Drew, on the other hand, just looked sort of annoyed.

"Oh, honey, no." Carrie was distracted by Layla as the toddler started playing with her chicken and making a mess.

With his mother seemingly done asking questions, Drew looked up and asked casually, "So, how long have you been gay?"

"Andrew," Jordan said with a glare, scolding him before taking another bite.

I coughed awkwardly, glancing down at the bare skin of my wrist as if it were a watch. I tapped it lightly with my finger. "About ten minutes, actually."

Jordan coughed violently, pounding on his chest with his fist. Whatever had been in his mouth must have gone down his throat unexpectedly. I watched his face turn beet red as his family all turned toward him with arched eyebrows.

"Jesus, Jordan. What did you do to the poor boy?" Drew teased.

"Okay," Jordan said, and pushed his chair back abruptly. He grabbed my arm, pulling me up from my seat. "Thanks for dinner, Mom, it was delicious. We're going to go study," he announced.

"Right. *Studying*." Drew winked suggestively as Jordan dragged me out of the dining room and back upstairs. He pulled me into his bedroom, closed the door, and held me there, my back pressed to the wood.

"Did you mean it?" he asked, his eyes desperately searching mine.

"What?" I asked, completely taken off guard by the situation. I was extremely aware of the tight, almost painful grip he kept on my upper arms.

"Have you made up your mind? Did you figure it out? Are you . . ."

"I think so," I responded, slightly terrified.

He immediately pulled me into a bone-crushing hug, cracking my back a little in the process. A joyful sound escaped his throat and Jordan lifted me into the air a bit, spinning us around in circles.

"You're gay!" he said, grinning as he let my feet touch the ground again, though he did not let me go.

"I—I'm gay," I said for the first time out loud. The words made me feel lighter in a way. I hadn't really realized it, but up until that point, it was as if there had been a giant hand squeezing me tighter and tighter from all sides. It had been building up this pressure inside of me to the point that I had nearly exploded. But now that I had finally said those words out loud, it was as if I was floating.

Jordan grabbed my face and planted a chaste kiss on my lips, and then immediately peppered the rest of my exposed skin with little kisses. I think he kissed every inch of my face before finally pulling me into another hug. He tucked my head under his chin and held me close.

"You have no idea how happy I am for you." I felt his chest vibrate as he spoke. I closed my eyes and listened to the steady rhythm of his heart. It was so soothing. I could've stayed right there forever.

After standing like that for a good while, I decided to break the silence. "Jordan?" I said into his chest.

"Mm-hmm?" he responded, though I felt it more than heard it.

"Can we, um, actually study? I *am* kind of behind in my classes right now."

"Way to kill the mood, Eli," he joked. He gave me a little breathing room. I looked up at him, grinning, and he pressed our foreheads together. "Of course we can. We can do whatever you want."

What do you want, Eli?

Jesus.

"Study. Yes, I want to study. Let's study," I repeated, more to remind myself than him. Pulling away from Jordan, and shaking other thoughts from my head, I grabbed my backpack off the floor and pulled out my AP Chemistry homework.

Jordan sat on the bed and scooted back until he was

leaning against the wall with his feet dangling over the edge. He patted the space next to him expectantly. I grabbed a pencil and a calculator from my bag before crawling up to join him. I leaned my head against his shoulder, his arm draped across mine, and looked down at the folder in my lap and started to work out the problems. Jordan offered input every now and then, usually when I forgot to do something, but mostly he just watched me with a small smile on his face.

If it was anybody else, I'd have found it creepy. Because it was Jordan, though, I didn't really mind. In fact, I kind of liked it.

"You forgot to convert that to grams," he whispered in my ear, making me pause and review my previous work. I flipped my pencil around and erased a few parts, then jabbed the numbers into my calculator and wrote down the converted digits before checking with him for approval. He nodded. I wrinkled my nose after reading through the next problem. It didn't make any sense. I read through it again and then looked up at him for help.

"You look cute when you make that face," he mused, gently kissing my finally-healed nose.

"It doesn't make sense," I said, ignoring his comment.

He pointed to my paper. "You have to subtract this volume from this one first."

"Oh," I said, looking at the problem again with new-found clarity. "I'm an idiot."

"No, you're not," he said, kissing my cheek. "You're perfect the way you are."

I was coming to find that Jordan was a very affectionate

person. It wasn't something that I was used to, as my parents had often been too busy to show us much affection when Ellie and I were growing up, but even still, it made me feel warm and fuzzy inside.

Accepting a compliment was new to me, but I said thank you, and then turned back to my work.

NO, I GOT THAT

I was actually pretty pleased with how much of my homework I was able to get caught up on while I was with Jordan. There were only a few more assignments for me to do before I was completely caught up from the days I'd missed because of the whole broken-nose-and-freaking-out-about-Jordan thing. It was already dark out, though, so instead of trying to work all night, I packed up my stuff.

"Done already?" Jordan asked with a hint of disappointment as he watched me zip up my backpack.

"It's getting late. I should be getting home."

Jordan pushed himself up off his bed. "Here, let me drive you."

"It's a short walk," I assured him.

"Yeah, but it's dark out," he argued. "I would feel better knowing you got home safely."

"I guess." I looked out the window as I slung my backpack over my shoulder. "As long as it's not an inconvenience for you."

"It's not," he said, grabbing his car keys from his desk and leading the way back downstairs.

Carrie spotted us heading for the front door. "Oh, are you leaving, honey?"

"Yes." I stopped briefly so I could talk to her. "Thanks for letting me stay for dinner. It was nice not having to cook it myself for once."

"It was a pleasure having you. You're welcome back here any time."

"Thank you again." I smiled politely. "Have a nice night."

"You too!" she said. With that, I went to the front door and followed Jordan outside.

Sitting in the passenger seat of his car a few moments later, I couldn't help but think about my recent revelation. I was gay. This boy made me want to be gay. This boy was gay. This boy was also *good* at being gay. Which was why I was now gay. Or had I always been gay?

"What are you thinking about?" Jordan asked as he drove.

"I have no clue," I said, shaking my head as I peered out the window. "Everything is going so fast through my mind that I can't pinpoint any one thought."

"Are they at least good thoughts?" he inquired.

"I think so," I said, though I sounded unsure.

"That's a positive." Try as he might, he couldn't keep the smile off of his face.

My eyes were drawn to the dimples in his cheeks, and I found myself fighting a small smile of my own. I forced my gaze back out the window.

A few seconds later, I felt Jordan's warm fingers snake underneath my palm. I held my breath as he slid the rest of his hand beneath mine and squeezed gently. He didn't let go either. I stared down at our joined hands and smiled. It was a nice, warm sensation, and I had no intention of breaking it.

Unfortunately, the ride back to my house wasn't far, and before long we found ourselves sitting in my driveway. I didn't want to get out of the car.

"So." Jordan turned and looked at me. "Does this count as a date?"

"This? A date?" I asked confusedly.

"I guess it's technically a study date." He grinned at me, dimples on full display.

"I'm not sure if that counts." I contemplated this notion as my eyes roamed over his beautiful facial features. Now that I had admitted to myself I was gay, it didn't feel as wrong for me to be checking him out.

"But if it was . . ." he said, dragging things out for dramatic effect, "wouldn't that mean I get to kiss you good-bye?"

My heart stuttered and my eyes snapped to his lips. Slowly, he leaned closer, over the center console. I felt his breath fan across my skin as my eyes slowly fluttered shut. But just as his lips brushed my own, there was an abrupt knock on the driver's-side window.

Jordan jerked away from me like I was a bucket of hot coals. He was panicked, fearing he'd just outed me to my family. His eyes went wide and he stuttered out an apology. "I'm sorry. I didn't see—"

I ducked my head to look outside and, seeing my sister there, felt all tension leave my body in a single, relieved sigh. "It's okay," I breathed. "She knows."

"How—" he began to ask, curious how Ellie could know anything when I myself had not known until only a few hours ago.

"She knows everything," I said, cutting him off. I quickly unbuckled my seat belt and leaned over both the center console and Jordan and pressed the button to roll down his window.

Ellie leaned over and peered through the window, gracing Jordan with a smile. "You must be Jordan." She stuck her hand through the window for a shake, but Jordan just sat there, frozen, as he laid eyes on the female version of yours truly for the very first time. "I'm Ellie, Elliot's twin sister."

"No, I got that." Jordan gestured to his own face, still in awe. "You look surprisingly similar."

Ellie didn't seem offended by that, thank God, but I wasn't just going to sit around and wait for Jordan to do something stupid. "Did you need something, El?" I asked with a hint of impatience. Judging by the take-out bags in both her hands, she had just been cleaning out our car.

She smirked at me and turned to Jordan again. "Since I'm sure he hasn't told you yet, Eli and I turn eighteen on December 8, and he is in desperate need of a companion to pull him away from the crazy relatives at our party. It's a Saturday. Will you come?"

"I have Holly," I objected.

"No, *I* have Holly. I've already invited her to be my

plus-one for this year, so you're fresh out of luck. Sorry, bud," she said, and shrugged indifferently, her focus shifting back to Jordan.

"You can't do that," I scoffed.

"Seniority." She gave me an evil grin.

"Four-minute seniority," I grumbled, crossing my arms.

"Look, Eli. If you don't want me to go . . ."

"It's not that. It's that—my family can be a little . . ." I trailed off, searching for the right word.

"Overwhelming," Ellie and I supplied at the same time.

Jordan glanced back and forth between us, taking in that rare moment of twin telepathy, before turning back to me. "If you can handle dinner with my family, I can handle a birthday party with yours."

"Don't say I didn't warn you," I said gravely, my mind flashing briefly to my nana. She was all kinds of crazy, and I feared what embarrassing things might pop out of her mouth once she met Jordan. She had absolutely no filter.

"When does it start?" Jordan asked my sister. He was a smart boy asking her, because I definitely wouldn't have told him.

"We're serving dinner at six, so I'd say five is probably a safe time for you to show up. There'll undoubtedly be relatives here before that, and Elliot will definitely need an excuse to get away from their interrogations by then," she informed him.

"Sounds good."

"See you then." She saluted him and then walked back toward the house.

Jordan rolled up his window and turned to me with a raised brow, but I was already halfway out of the car.

"Thanks for helping me figure things out," I told him, hoping he caught the double meaning in my statement. "I'll see you tomorrow."

"What? No good-bye kiss?"

I closed the car door and playfully flipped him off through the glass before heading over to the front door. Even from within his car, I could hear his laughter.

I watched as he backed out of my driveway, a smile creeping across my lips. I waited until I could no longer see his car before finally turning back around and heading inside. Ellie was on the living room couch, and she gave me a knowing smirk when our eyes met. I just sent her a playful glare in return.

After shutting the door behind me, I kicked off my shoes, greeted the rest of my family, and made my way up to my room.

I plopped down onto my unmade bed and stared up at my ceiling as the events of today replayed behind my eyes. How had I ignored the butterflies before?

They were so painfully obvious.

I DON'T KNOW, CAN YOU?

It was finally the weekend again. Today's lab had gone just as well as the previous ones Jordan and I had done. Everything went smoothly and quickly, and we were once again finished with our work early and confident in the answers we'd gotten. I truly had never had such a great lab partner before.

I glanced over at him. He was driving me home again, which was supernice—I hadn't had to ride the school bus for weeks. There wasn't much in the world that was better than the revelation that you didn't need to ride the school bus. At least for me. Those things were nothing but loud, chaotic, and annoying—too many screaming kids who refused to sit down in their seats.

Jordan seemed lost in thought as he stared out at the road ahead. I could tell—he had that look on his face that he got when he was thinking about something really hard. It was difficult to spot if you didn't know him very well, but I could see it in the way his eyebrows drew slightly together

and how his eyes narrowed. I wondered what he was thinking about. Maybe something was bothering him.

Luckily, I didn't have to wait long to find out.

"Hey," he said as we came to a stop at a red light. I
turned and looked at him, glimpsing both nervousness and
uncertainty in his eyes. "Can I take you out on a date?"

Heat spread to my cheeks as I looked out the car window again. We hadn't really been on any official dates yet;
we'd just sort of been hanging out here and there when we
could. I had never been on a date, though, so I wasn't really
sure what to expect.

"I don't know, can you?" I asked after a few seconds,
resorting to correcting his grammar instead of giving him
an answer. I glanced back at him and caught him staring out
at the road with a small grin.

"Oh, I can do a lot of things," Jordan responded, his
tone suggestive.

I blushed deeper at that. My mind went all the way into
the gutter and I turned my head even more toward the window to try to hide this. I knew it was useless, though. He
could likely still see the redness on my neck and ears.

Jordan laughed at me then. I pouted, glaring at him.
"I'm not answering until you use proper grammar."

"*May* I take you out on a date?"

"That's not a very memorable way to ask someone out.
Green light," I teased.

But Jordan didn't look at the light. He continued to stare
at me, even as cars behind us started honking their horns.

"Jordan. Green light," I said again, growing anxious as
the people behind us got even more fed up.

"I'm not going until you say yes," he said.

"Okay, yes, fine," I said, turning around in my seat to glance out the back window. "Just go already."

At my answer, he took his foot off of the brake and drove through the intersection. Every one of the cars behind us, however, got caught by the next red light.

"You're such an asshole," I mumbled, facing forward again.

"That may be true, but at least I'm an asshole who has a date with you," he said with a cocky grin.

I sank lower in my seat and mumbled, "I would've said yes either way."

"What was that?" he asked, though, by the look on his face, I knew that he'd heard me.

"I'm not repeating that," I grumbled and looked out the window again. "Jordan, you went past my house already."

"I know," he said, still smiling.

"What do you mean, you know?"

"I'm taking you on a date," he stated very matter of factly, as if this was supposed to be obvious to me.

"Now?" I asked, a million thoughts flying through my head all at once.

"Yes. Is there something wrong with that?" he asked with false innocence.

"No, it's just—I was expecting a little time to mentally prepare myself."

"Oh, there's no way in hell I'm giving you time to freak out about this and change your mind."

"You have so much faith in me."

"I've been in your shoes, Eli," he reminded me.

"We wear the same size?" I smirked.

"Shut up." He shoved my shoulder playfully.

After a few moments I asked, "So where are we going?"

"It's a secret." He wiggled his eyebrows at me.

"Really?" I said, ignoring his silliness.

"Really, really."

"Fine." I relented. As I watched the scenery pass by, I noticed that he was taking us north. There were a few bigger towns up this way, and by bigger, I meant that they had actual storefronts and more than one gas station, unlike Pinecrest, which was mostly dead. Downtown only had about three shops still open. The rest were empty, either having gone out of business or having moved to somewhere more profitable. The only things left were a thrift shop, a bookstore, and a bar. There were a couple of places to eat outside of downtown, like Uncle Tony's Pizzeria and Georgie's Diner, but other than that, there was absolutely nothing in Pinecrest.

I didn't have much reason to come north in my day-to-day life, but on occasion, my mother would take us school shopping at the mall up in Cooper Creek. I felt lighter when I recalled a memory of Ellie and me messing around in Walmart and making fun of the silly products we came across.

By the looks of it, that was where we were heading now. The mall anyway, not Walmart.

The speed limit dropped to twenty-five miles per hour as we got closer to town, and I watched as rows of houses bled into a downtown shopping district, nervous excitement building in my stomach.

After a while, Jordan pulled into the parking lot of Fun Zone, one of the biggest arcades in the area. It had a trampoline park, a bowling alley, and a pretty intense multiple-story laser-tag arena. I hadn't been inside the place since my thirteenth birthday, but I felt excitement coursing through my veins at the prospect of going in again.

"Well?" Jordan turned to me. "What are we waiting for?"

I matched his smile, unbuckled my seat belt, and flung open the door. Jordan was soon walking beside me. My breath caught in my throat as his warm hand slipped into mine. I looked down at our linked fingers and felt my stomach flip a little.

"Is this okay?" he asked, squeezing my hand for emphasis.

"Um . . ." I noticed the rapid thumping of my heart against my rib cage as I did a quick scan of the parking lot. We were in a different town now. What were the chances that someone we knew would see us? What were the chances of someone we knew seeing us and even caring?

"Elliot?" Jordan asked, drawing me out of my thoughts.

And I decided, in that moment, that I loved the warmth radiating from his palm and that I didn't care if anyone saw us. I tightened my grip on his hand. "Yes. It's perfect."

And with that, Jordan led me inside for our very first date.

I'M COMING FOR YOU

I could feel my heart beating heavily as I rounded a corner, eyes straining to see in the dark. The walls of the narrow halls around me were painted black, with graffiti that glowed in bright neon colors under the black lights above. I made my way up the ramp to the second level and peered through oddly shaped holes in the walls in search of movement. I wasn't sure where Jordan was at the moment, so I gripped my plastic laser gun tightly and rounded another corner.

The idiot had insisted we be on different teams, so now not only did I have to worry about hyperactive, unsupervised ten-year-olds but also a full-sized, scary-as-hell teen boy who was no doubt hunting me down at that exact moment. Coming around another corner, I flinched as a boy half my height from the red team shot at my vest. I shot back, my laser gun vibrating with every hit, and luckily was able to duck out of sight before my vest powered down.

I was on the yellow team. Jordan was on blue. I had yet

to come across anyone on the green team, but I was sure they were around here somewhere.

Hearing the cringe-worthy yet iconic sounds of laser guns up ahead, I rushed forward and peeked around the corner. There were three young kids, each from a different team, engaged in a full-out battle in the section of the arena that I had just wandered into. A small boy wearing blue was crouched behind the free-standing rock-shaped obstacle closest to me. Another boy was on the other side of the room, and I could only tell that he was on the green team because of a small bit of his vest that lit up through one of the small holes in the wall he was hiding behind. I spotted a little brown-haired girl from the red team in the other corner. She was watching the other two as if her life depended on it. Based on their similar ages and the way they interacted with each other, I guessed that they were friends. Maybe even siblings.

None of them had noticed me yet. I tried to shield my vest behind the corner and aimed my laser gun at the clearest shot: the unsuspecting kid from the blue team. He seemed confused as to why he was taking damage at first, but once he figured out it was me, he hurried to find a different hiding place safe from my aim while also trying his best to shoot back at me. My vest vibrated a couple of times, meaning he had met his mark with a few of his blind shots. I backed up, trying to move out of his range.

I backed into something I couldn't see and jumped, but didn't have a chance to turn around before an arm snaked around my waist and lifted me up a few inches. I squealed in surprise and immediately recognized the laugh that followed.

"Jordan!" I growled as he carried me out into the open, using my body as a shield while he shot at the other boys. My vest vibrated as the kids shot at us. After taking a few hits, there was a long vibration before my vest and gun powered down altogether.

"Jordan! You killed me!" I exclaimed, looking down to see my vest counting down from fifteen; I'd be reinstated in a few seconds, but Jordan still wasn't dropping me. "Let go of me!" I tried to wiggle out of his hold, but he just laughed and kept shooting. "This is against the rules! Let me go!"

"What do I get out of it?" he asked, his lips precariously close to my ear.

"Uh—" The words died on my tongue. I turned my head slightly.

"What will you give me, Eli?" He grinned, letting my feet touch the ground again, though he still did not move his arm from around my waist.

"Bragging rights?" I tried.

He tightened his hold on me and shook his head. "Try again."

I started to panic. My vest lit up again. "How about a kiss? Later." My words were quiet, since I didn't really want the other kids to hear, but Jordan heard them just fine.

With a wide grin, he whispered in my ear, "Deal." With that, he let me go and immediately started shooting at me. I raised my gun and shot at him as well, backing up to find cover.

"You better run, Eli. I'm coming for you," he called from around the corner. My eyes widened at his choice of words and I cursed under my breath as I stumbled a bit. Thanks to Jordan, my vest was close to powering down again—I had only one more reboot before I was out of the game for good.

I managed to fend him off until the game timed out and ended. All at once, the lights brightened and everyone's vests powered down. Jordan found me then and threw his arm over my shoulders, laughing. "I haven't had that much fun in a long time."

"Me neither." I grinned, panting as the adrenaline left me. Jordan and I followed the blinking lights on the floor back to the main room, where we removed our vests and hung them up before exiting out to the lobby.

Jordan pulled out his phone and checked the time. "Let's see," he said, glancing at the time on his home screen. "It's four thirty now. How about we play some arcade games for an hour or so and then go get something to eat?"

"That sounds like a good plan." I nodded, tilting my head in consideration. "But I have a suggestion."

"And what's that?" he asked curiously.

"I want to teach you how to cook something."

"Me? Cook?" he said sarcastically, placing a hand over his heart. "Do you *want* food poisoning?"

"It's not that hard," I assured him. "And I'll be there to help you the whole time."

He seemed lost in thought as we walked out to the arcade area. "What would we make?"

I was silent for a moment, glancing up as I tried to visualize what we could make from the ingredients that were currently in my house. I ran over a few different ideas in my mind and dismissed the ones I considered to be a little too complex.

"We could stop and get a few things at the store to make homemade pizzas," I suggested, watching his face to gauge his reaction.

"I like pizza," he said, looking down at me. "As long as you're there to make sure I don't kill anyone or burn anything down, then I'm open to try anything."

"Looks like we're having pizza then." I smiled at him. "Come on. Let's go play some games."

"What do you want to play?" Jordan asked, looking around at all the different options available to us.

"I don't know," I said. "I'm terrible at making decisions."

"Let's get some tokens first."

"Right." I fished in my pocket for my wallet.

"I'll get it," Jordan insisted, his wallet already out as he walked up to one of the machines that dispensed tokens. He inserted a twenty-dollar bill into the machine. "Ten bucks each should be enough for an hour, right?"

"It should be," I said. "I'm not really sure, though. It's been a while since I've been to an arcade."

"If it's not enough, we can always get more," he pointed out.

"That's true," I agreed, watching as the little coins filled the tray at the bottom of the machine. Jordan scooped them up and took a moment to make sure they were divided evenly before handing me my half. He put his coins in his pockets, so I did the same, and we looked around, trying to figure out what to play first.

"How about that basketball game?" Jordan pointed to one of those large, free-standing machines where you shot as many balls as you could into the baskets.

"You have far too much faith in my hand-eye coordination," I said. "But sure."

Jordan chuckled. "There's two of them right next to each other. Want to make it a competition?"

"I'm definitely going to die," I said, but followed him anyway.

Jordan and I put our coins in at the same time. The miniature basketballs rolled out and we started throwing them at our individual baskets.

"This is rigged!" I complained, most of my shots just bouncing off the rim when they looked like they were going to go in. I had only made one basket so far, but Jordan had made three. I threw another and it went in. My next one bounced off the rim but actually came back to me instead of going down the ramp and out of play, so I technically got a free shot with it.

"You could still beat me," Jordan said, throwing another ball and missing completely.

I had a feeling there weren't many shots left before the machine would hold back the balls, demanding more tokens from us. I took a moment to prepare myself and, after taking a deep breath, surprisingly made another basket.

We were tied.

My last three balls, however, missed their mark completely, so it really didn't make that much of a difference. Jordan sank one more basket on his last shot and ended up winning anyway. I pouted a little, but by the time we'd collected our tickets at the end of the game, I had already forgotten my loss and was excited to move on to whatever was next.

"Oh my gosh, I love Skee-Ball!" I said, practically dragging Jordan across the room when I spotted the machines on the opposite wall. I didn't even wait for him to put tokens in his own game before I had mine ready to go.

To be honest, I wasn't really sure why I liked Skee-Ball so much. Maybe it was the weight of the balls, or the fact that it was basically bowling, but without pins and with a smaller ball. I rolled the first ball straight down the lane, or whatever it was called, and it landed in the fifty-point hole at the end. The next ball I aimed diagonally so that I could get it to the hundred-point hole, but unfortunately, just missed, and the ball ended up rolling down to a ten-pointer instead. The next roll, however, I got the hundred. And then the next one, and the one after that

"Wow, you're really good at this one," Jordan said, sounding impressed.

"Aren't you going to play?" I asked, noticing he hadn't put any tokens in the machine beside mine.

"Nah," he said. "I don't want to embarrass myself."

"Oh, come on," I said as I collected the tickets coming out of my machine. "You made me play the basketball game. Besides, I won't judge you. I'll even start another game if you want."

"Fine," Jordan sighed, putting in his tokens. I started another round and smiled as Jordan only made it into the ten-point holes, along with a few forty-pointers.

"Now what?" I said as I collected more tickets.

"Want to try to get one of those giant plastic balls from that claw machine?" he asked, pointing to the nearby glass case filled with stuffed animals and various trinkets.

"Sure," I said, and followed him over to it. We each took turns: one person moving the claw while the other stood just off to the side, directing how much farther to move it.

It took us a couple of tries, but we each won a ball. Mine was blue and had little plastic spikes all over it; Jordan's was the same but purple.

We played a few more games before we finally ran out of tokens. We walked up to the prize counter, laughing together, and handed our tickets to the guy working there. He counted them up by running them through a machine, and then Jordan picked out his prize. He chose a bouncy ball and a Chinese finger trap, and then, to my surprise, donated the rest of his tickets to me. In that moment, I realized I was having fun. I wasn't thinking about Cole or what happened earlier or anything other than being with Jordan and being myself. I didn't hate this at all. In fact, I could get used to it.

"Get something good," he said.

Adding Jordan's tickets to my total, I backed up a little and considered my options. I really was terrible at making decisions. After debating a while, I decided to get a pair of sunglasses, a slingshot, and a little foam airplane glider. All told, we'd spent a little over an hour playing games, but still had time to get back and start making dinner.

"Hungry?" Jordan asked as we walked back out to the parking lot.

"I could eat," I said as we approached his car.

Instead of getting in behind the wheel, Jordan followed me to the passenger side and grabbed my wrist to stop me from getting in. "Does this count as later?" he asked with a cheeky grin.

I scowled at him. We hadn't even left yet and he was already asking for his "payment."

"Don't give me that look," I said, and then scowled at him as he pulled a puppy dog face on me. I tried to ignore the absolute adorableness of it all. He could probably make me do anything with that face—and frankly, that kind of concerned me. He stepped into my vision, forcing me to look up into his pleading eyes.

Ack! I couldn't do it! I couldn't resist!

With an annoyed sigh, I leaned forward, tilted my head, and pressed my lips to his. I felt him smile against me as our lips touched. Euphoria spread through me and my annoyance diminished. How did this one boy have so much power over me? Why did I find that fact all the more exhilarating?

We slowly drew apart and I looked up into his eyes once again. I wanted to kiss him a second time, but then remembered we were in a public place and still had things we needed to do. I ushered him back to his side of the car and then returned to the passenger side and got in myself. "We need to stop at the grocery store to pick up a few things."

"Okay," he said, buckling his seat belt. "I hope I don't burn anything down trying to cook this pizza."

"Don't worry." I smiled at him. "I won't let anything bad happen."

NOW WE WAIT

"What exactly are we looking for?" Jordan asked as we entered the grocery store.

"Powdered pizza dough mix, pepperoni, and pizza sauce." I counted the items off on my fingers. "I'm pretty sure I already have shredded mozzarella and vegetable oil at home."

"This is already more complicated than I thought it would be." He looked scared.

"It'll be fine, I promise." I led him down one of the aisles, where I suspected the pizza crust mix might be located. It only took a few minutes of perusal before I found what I was looking for and grabbed three packages, checking the directions on the back to be sure I wasn't missing any of the ingredients.

"All right," I said, handing the boxes to Jordan. "You can carry these."

He did not object. Then I led him down the next aisle to look for the pizza sauce. There were a lot of cans of different tomato-based sauces, but I ended up finding some specifically stated to be pizza sauce. I debated in my head for a moment before deciding that two cans of pizza sauce would be enough to make three pizzas.

"Okay, we have pizza crust and pizza sauce," I said, turning to Jordan. "Now we just need pepperoni. Are there any other toppings you'd like on your pizza that I might not have at home?"

"I'm not picky," he said with a shrug. It was very unhelpful.

"We're going to make some classic pepperoni pizzas then," I told him. "And anything else depends on what I can find in my house."

"Okay."

"All right." I carried the sauces in one arm. "Onward to the pepperoni." Down the next aisle I found a small package of pepperoni relatively quickly. We went to check out then and were back in Jordan's car soon after.

"To your house next?" he asked, making sure I didn't need to stop anywhere else first.

"Yep," I said, glancing at my phone. We still had enough time to get everything done so that it'd be ready by the time my family got home from work and school. Hopefully, they would all be ready to eat—I planned on making three pizzas in the event that my entire family actually made it home on time.

It wasn't long before Jordan pulled into my driveway. I hopped out of the car and grabbed the grocery bag out of the back seat. Jordan followed close behind as I made my way up to the front door. It was still locked, seeing as no one was home yet, so I reached for the spare key we kept hidden on the ledge above the door and unlocked it.

"I guess I know how to break into your house now," Jordan joked as I replaced the key.

"Shut up," I said playfully and led him inside.

This was his first time inside, and I couldn't help but become immediately self-conscious about every little thing about my house. Was it too messy? Was it too clean? Had we left anything out in the open that might be embarrassing?

"Is this one you?" Jordan asked. I turned to see him looking at an old photo hanging on the wall of Ellie and me when we were toddlers. We were on some teeter-totter at a park somewhere. It wasn't the one down the road, that much I knew. It might've been from when we had been out of town visiting family at the time—I couldn't remember.

"Yeah," I said as I kicked off my shoes, leaving them by the door with all of the other pairs. "I'm on the left. Ellie is on the right."

"You're so cute!"

"Aren't all kids supposed to be cute?" I asked, watching as he took his shoes off as well.

"Not necessarily," he said, straightening up again. "Andrew was really ugly when he was little."

I snorted a little and slapped his shoulder. "You shouldn't say that about your brother!" I said, halfheartedly scolding him.

"It's true, though."

I shook my head and led Jordan into the kitchen. I set the grocery bag down on the counter. "Shall we get started?"

"Yes." Jordan clapped his hands together once but seemed to have no idea what getting started entailed.

"First step to cooking anything is to wash your hands," I said.

"Right," he said, and walked over to the kitchen sink.

I took the ingredients we'd purchased out of the plastic bag and put the bag in a drawer with some others we kept for recycling while I waited for him to finish. I quickly washed my own hands and then rooted around in the cupboards, finding what we would need and setting it all on the counter. My nerves had quieted down considerably now that I was in the familiar setting of my kitchen, but they were still present.

"Grab one of those packages of crust mix," I told him. "There are directions on the back." He did as instructed while I took three decently large bowls out and set them on the counter.

"It says to add half a cup of warm water and let it sit somewhere warm for a few minutes." He looked up at me.

"Okay, so empty each package into one of these bowls and then add half a cup of warm water to each one," I told him. He nodded, opened up the packages, and poured a powdered mix into each bowl.

"Does it matter how warm the water is?"

"The hotter the better," I said. "It's supposed to activate the yeast. Think of it as chemistry."

"Chemistry?" Jordan perked up a bit at the mention of science. "What does cooking have to do with chemistry?"

"Quite a bit, actually," I said. "You add precise measurements of different things together to create the desired reactions. In this instance, the hot water is acting as a catalyst for the yeast. The yeast will in turn cause the dough to expand with carbon dioxide air bubbles so that the dough is less chewy and more airy or fluffy."

"Well, shit. I've never thought of it like that before."

"The greatest part is that the end result is food instead of chemicals."

"Food is always a win," he agreed, patting his stomach affectionately before moving to get some hot water.

I smiled lightly at him while getting out the sauce, shredded mozzarella, and anything else we might want to use as toppings and placing it all on the counter.

Jordan stood at the kitchen sink with his finger under the running water so he could tell how hot it was getting. Once satisfied, he filled up the measuring cup and carefully walked it over to the first bowl, trying not to spill any of it. I tried not to laugh at him for taking the water all the way to the bowl instead of just taking the bowl closer to the water.

"Here," I said, handing him a wooden spoon. "Mix that one up so that it can sit while you work on the others."

"Yes, sir," he said, accepting the utensil and getting to work. "Oh my gosh, it's turning into dough." I smiled at his revelation. Carrie hadn't been kidding: he really hadn't cooked much before.

"Is this good?" he asked.

I looked into the bowl and nodded. "Yep. Get started on the next one," I said, pulling out a clean hand towel and placing it over the bowl. After preheating the oven, I put the bowl on top of the stove so that it would hopefully warm up a little with the oven on beneath it.

Jordan repeated the process twice more, and by the time he'd finished mixing the last bowl, the first one had risen enough to start on the next step.

"Now what?" he asked as he set the third bowl on top of the stove with the others.

"Grab the first one," I said while pulling out a circular pizza pan and a bag of flour. I first wiped off the countertop with a wet dishcloth to make sure it was clean and then proceeded to sprinkle some flour on top of the counter. Then I grabbed Jordan's hands and covered them with flour as well. "Have you ever kneaded dough before?"

"Sometimes I feel like I need cookie dough," he said.

I shook my head. I would've covered my face with my hands if they weren't currently covered in flour. "Knead with a *k*, not the other word for want."

"Oh. Then no."

I took the towel off the bowl and plopped the dough onto the floured countertop. "Okay, well, the flour is to stop the dough from sticking to your hands. What you want to do is kind of move the dough around. Press into it, fold it onto itself, basically just work with it. If your hands start to stick, put some more flour on them."

"Okay," Jordan said, and after watching me do it a few times, he started to do it on his own. I observed him for a moment to make sure he didn't need any more help before I floured some more space beside him and grabbed the second bowl of dough.

"How long do we do this for?" he asked.

"It depends," I said. "For this, it doesn't need to be too long. We're just trying to make sure the pizza crust isn't too flat or tough. Let me see how yours is." I took his dough and kneaded it a few more times before determining that it was ready for the next step. "This is good," I said, moving over to the pizza pan. "So, for this part, we need to grease the pan and our hands so that we can shape the dough into a crust. I'm out of nonstick spray, so we're just going to use vegetable oil."

After greasing the pan, I taught Jordan how to press the dough and stretch it to fit the shape of the pan. While he did that, I worked on the remaining dough. I only had two circular pizza pans, so the third one ended up on a rectangular cookie sheet.

"Now we need to precook this crust for a few minutes," I said, grabbing an oven mitt and transferring the completed crusts to the oven. "And then all that's left is putting on the sauce, cheese, and toppings, and then baking it."

"Doesn't sound so bad," Jordan said as he rinsed his hands off in the sink.

"See, I told you." I cleaned up the flour on the counter. When the timer went off a few minutes later, I pulled each of the pans out of the oven and set them on top of the burners to cool. Then I moved all of the topping-type items to the island and found a can opener for the pizza sauce. By the time I'd finished, the crusts had cooled enough to put toppings on. I brought them over to the open space on the island and gave Jordan a spoon. "You can spread the pizza sauce around with this. Try to make sure it covers everything fairly evenly, and that you get the sauce up close to the edge."

"Okay," he said, and got to work. I poured half of the

first can of sauce onto his crust and then the other half of it onto mine. After that, it was time for the cheese. We had a giant bag of shredded mozzarella, so there wasn't much danger of running out. I also didn't have to give Jordan much instruction for this part—it was pretty self-explanatory.

It wasn't long before we had two nicely assembled pepperoni pizzas. I ended up adding some minced garlic and garlic pepper to mine as well, but Jordan's stayed simple. After popping them in the oven, we assembled the third pizza together.

"How do you like cooking?" I asked as I sprinkled mozzarella onto the last pizza.

"It's not as bad as I thought it was going to be," he admitted. "Dare I say it might have even been fun."

I smiled as I watched him place pepperoni slices at even intervals all over the pizza. "That's good."

"How much time do they need to cook?" he asked.

"The first pizzas should be out in twelve minutes or so. I'll have to keep an eye on them since they are both in there at the same time. One may take a little longer than the other. We can put the third one in when those are done." Jordan nodded. I glanced at the time. "It's almost six fifteen. My family should be getting home any minute."

"Cool." He leaned against the counter. "So now we wait?"

"Yep," I confirmed. "Now we wait."

Two minutes later, the front door opened and a voice called out, "Something smells good!"

I looked up as my dad poked his head around the corner into the kitchen. He was the first one home.

"Hi, Dad," I greeted him, glancing back at my phone, the timer counting down with painful efficiency. I tried to keep my voice level, with normal, nothing-to-see-here calm. "How was work?"

"Good, good," he said as he walked into the kitchen. He was dressed in a suit and tie, and his short blond hair was neatly combed away from his face. My sister and I had both inherited his hair, but unfortunately, neither of us had inherited his ability to control it.

My dad set his eyes on Jordan then, who was currently sitting on one of the stools at the kitchen island. "Hi. I don't think we've met. I'm Peter."

"Hi, Peter." Jordan smiled politely and shook my father's hand. "I'm Jordan. It's nice to meet you."

"Nice to meet you too," he said, smiling back. He turned back to me. "Is your mother home yet?"

"No," I told him. "You're the first one."

"Cool," he said. "I'm going to go change out of these clothes. How much longer until food?"

"Just a few more minutes," I assured him. He gave me two thumbs-ups before disappearing up the stairs. I released a shaky breath. I hadn't really thought about Jordan meeting my parents, but it was too late now to turn back. I could only pray that this whole thing didn't end in a train wreck.

Ellie came through the front door a few minutes later. I was about to say hi, but just as I opened my mouth, the timer went off. I turned around and grabbed the oven mitt to take the pizzas out of the oven. I checked the one on the bottom rack and determined that it needed a few more minutes before it was done; however, the other one was ready, so I pulled it out and set it on top of the stove to cool.

"Hey, Jordan," she said when she spotted him.

"Hey," he said, waving back as she darted upstairs, backpack in tow.

I took the second pizza out of the oven just as my dad came back downstairs. I put in the last pizza and set the timer. "Hey, can you get out some plates and stuff?" I asked him.

"Sure thing, kiddo," he said. "Are you staying for dinner, Jordan?"

"If you don't mind," he said with a smile.

"Not at all." Dad turned back to me. "Oh, and your mother just texted. She's running a little late and should be back in a half hour at most."

"Okay." I got out the pizza cutter. Dad grabbed a stack of plates before disappearing into the dining room to set the table.

"Your dad seems nice," Jordan said once my dad was out of earshot.

"Yeah," I said, rolling the pizza cutter through the first pizza in straight lines. "He is."

Dad came back in then, raiding the silverware drawer for some utensils. Then he tore off several sheets of paper towel to use as napkins before disappearing again. When he returned a third time it was to grab us all some water.

"Would you like a water, Jordan?" he asked as he started filling up glasses at the sink.

"Sure, I'd love one."

Ellie reappeared moments later. "Is dinner starting soon?" she asked, entering the kitchen.

"Yes," I said.

"Good. I've got a paper due at midnight." She picked up a couple of the waters Dad had filled and carried them to the table in the dining room.

"Welp," I said, turning to Jordan. "I think everything is ready."

"Awesome." He stood up from his stool.

The two of us entered the dining room. "Dinner is ready," I told the other two. Then we took our plates back to the kitchen and grabbed ourselves a few slices of pizza before returning to the dining room and taking our seats. Jordan sat beside me, Ellie across from me, and my father at the head of the table like he normally did. There was a seat left open for my mother next to my father and across from Jordan. I'd never had a friend over for dinner before—Holiday didn't count—and I was surprised at how *easy* it was, how fun it was to have a full house and not to be sitting in my room eating by myself, the rest of my family busy—with good reason, but busy nonetheless.

"Wow, this is really good," Jordan said after he took his first bite.

I glanced at the piece in his hands and couldn't spot any black from the garlic pepper seasoning I'd put on mine. "That's the one you made."

"Really?" he seemed even more surprised. "Which one did you make?"

I looked at the other pieces on his plate and pointed to the one that had visible seasoning and minced garlic on it. "That one."

He took a bite of that one next and nodded to himself. "This one is definitely better."

"Neither of them is bad," my father said. Ellie agreed.

There were a few minutes of silence as we ate, and then my father set down one of his pieces and said, "So, does anyone have any amusing anecdotes for the day?"

Jordan glanced at me for a translation. I whispered, "A story or incident."

"Ah."

"My sociology professor forgot about the quiz we were supposed to have today," Ellie told him.

"That's no good," he said. "You're supposed to be learning."

"She lectured the whole class time." Ellie shrugged. "So technically, I was still learning."

"I guess." He looked at me next. "What about you, Elliot?"

"I taught Jordan how to cook a pizza," I said, looking over at Jordan.

"Well, he did a good job. You must've been a good teacher." My father praised us both.

I smiled and took another bite, hoping that he would stop talking to me and move on.

"Jordan?" he said.

Jordan looked up. "Oh . . . I cooked for the first time today."

"Really? This was your first time cooking anything?" my father asked.

"Yeah," Jordan confirmed. "It was surprisingly fun."

"You're already better at it than I am."

"That's not saying much," Ellie said, snickering.

The timer for the last pizza went off then. I quickly wiped my mouth and excused myself to go get it. My mother walked in right as I pulled it out of the oven.

"Hey, Mom. Dinner's ready. My friend Jordan's here."

"Oh, thank you," she said as she removed her jacket and hung it on the hook by the front door. "Wait—"

Not giving any time to explain, I cut the new pizza quickly into slices before returning to the table. "Mom's home," I said.

"Hi, honey!" Dad shouted loud enough that the neighbors probably heard it. I cringed.

Mom glared at him from around the corner, but Dad just chuckled and continued eating. She finished removing her shoes and came in and grabbed her plate from the table. Then she went and got herself some food.

"Oh—sorry. Elliot just told me your name, but whoosh, already gone?" my mother said when she returned to the table and noticed Jordan sitting beside me.

"Jordan Hughes, ma'am. I'm Elliot's friend from school."

"Oh please, none of that formal stuff. It makes me feel old." She scrunched up her nose in distaste.

"You *are* old, honey," Dad teased with a smirk.

My mother sent him a fierce glare, looking like she wanted to smack him upside the head, though she thankfully refrained from doing so in the presence of company. Huffing in frustration, she turned her gaze back to Jordan. "You can call me Loraine," she said.

"It's a pleasure to meet you." He smiled politely.

My mother seemed pleased with his manners, and

M. MONTGOMERY

once she had taken her first bite, she continued to question Jordan about his life.

"Are you a senior this year as well?" she asked curiously.

"Yes," Jordan said. "I recently transferred to Pinecrest."

"Where from?"

"Hanover, New Hampshire."

"Oh wow. That's quite far away. What do you think of Michigan so far?"

"I'm really liking it," Jordan told her, seeming to recall some of his memories fondly. "It's not a lot different from Hanover, so it already feels a lot like home."

"Glad to hear it. Where are you living?"

"Just down the road, actually. I'm in the white house with the old wooden swing set out front."

"Oh!" my mother's eyes lit up in recognition. "You're the ones who moved into Donna and Lee's old place?"

Jordan shrugged. "I guess. I don't know the previous owners."

My mother nodded to herself as if confirming her own statement. "Yeah, they were an older couple. They decided to move down to Florida so they didn't have to deal with the snow anymore."

"That's understandable," Jordan said. "I've heard Michigan winters are pretty intense."

"They're even worse in the Upper Peninsula. Since we're pretty centralized in the Lower Peninsula, we don't get as many lake-effect snowstorms," my dad added.

"I bet." Jordan nodded and then laughed. "My mom is still having trouble grasping the concept that there are two parts to Michigan."

"In her defense, there's not much up there. And geographically Michigan looks like it's two different states."

"She'll figure it out eventually." He shrugged it off. "I knew about Upper Michigan before we moved here because of researching colleges."

"Oh, which colleges were you looking at?" My mother's interest perked up a little more, as did my father's.

"Up there? Michigan Tech. I've been looking at University of Michigan and Michigan State, too, but I think Tech is my top choice at this point."

"Really? We're both Michigan Tech alumni." My father grinned and gestured between my mother and himself. "What are you thinking about majoring in?"

"Chemical engineering, I think," he said.

"I was a mechanical engineering major," my mom said.

"And I was an accounting major with a minor in economics," my dad said.

"That's really cool! What was your favorite thing about Tech?" Jordan asked both of my parents.

"I really liked the atmosphere," my mother said. "It has this small-town vibe where everybody knows everybody."

My father nodded in agreement before tacking on, "And it's very safe. During the winters, it's too cold for anyone to do anything but stay inside and study, so there's not really anything sketchy happening up there."

"Makes sense." Jordan nodded. "I suppose that's also why it has such a reputation for having good students."

I was surprised by how easily Jordan fell into conversation with both my parents. Then again, I probably should've known he would. He was a friendly person regardless, but he actually happened to have something in common with both of them. He and my mom hit it off because of his interest in engineering, and I expected he and my dad would get along because of their shared love of soccer.

Though I was quiet for most of dinner, I enjoyed listening to the conversations they were having. At one point, I looked up and noticed Ellie giving me a knowing smile. I blushed and looked down, focusing on my meal instead of her.

At least now I knew that my family liked him.

WORTHLESS

I had completely forgotten about the reading I had to do for English lit, so I walked down the hallway the next day with my nose buried in my textbook, furiously trying to catch up. I had only a few pages left and knew I'd probably be able to finish up in the first few minutes of class.

I was just reaching the climax of the short story—where the man was about to be killed in a fighting arena in front of the woman he loved—when the book was suddenly wrenched out of my hands and flung across the hallway. I looked up to see Morgan in front of me. He shoved me to the side, slamming me into the lockers there. Then Nate, appearing to one side, grabbed me by my shirt and yanked me into the bathroom, practically tossing me inside. I skidded across the tiled floor and Morgan, Nate, and now Cole, too, followed me in. Cole shut the bathroom door and stood in front of it, effectively blocking anyone wanting to get in or out.

"What do you guys want?" I propped myself up on my

elbows and glared up at them. I didn't try to get all the way up, though—I had learned that lesson the hard way.

Morgan snickered and stalked forward, gripping the front of my shirt and hauling me to my feet. "I want you to scream for your boyfriend," he said, laughing before slamming me up against the wall and holding me there.

"What's your freaking problem, huh?" I growled. I couldn't stand it anymore; I couldn't just sit idly by and let them walk all over me. I pushed against Morgan's chest and spat, "Get away from me!"

He looked surprised that I'd had the audacity to actually stand up to him. I didn't waste a second of this brief opportunity and bolted for the door. But Nate was there before I was and blocked me with a shove, sending me face to face with Morgan again. Nate closed the gap behind me—they had me covered from both sides.

"You think you're invincible now, Goldman?" Morgan sneered and stepped forward, getting in my face again. I held my ground.

"You don't know shit about me."

"Don't I?" he said, taunting me, an evil glint in his eye. "I know that there's nothing special about you. I know that your family loves your sister more than they love you. You're just a disappointment to them."

"Stop it, Morgan," I warned, though I couldn't keep my voice from shaking.

"They already have a perfect daughter. Why should they love you?"

I took a step back and looked away, tears pooling in my eyes, burning.

"How could your mother ever love a fag like you?"

"Stop," I choked out.

"How could *anyone* love such a disappointment?"

"Stop!" I screamed, and swung hard with my fist, striking Morgan in the face. Nate responded by immediately tackling me to the floor. Luckily, I had the common sense to raise my head before it smacked into the tile, but the body that landed on top of me caused quite a bit of pain. I groaned and tried to push Nate off of me. He didn't budge.

"Hold him down," Morgan instructed, wiping some blood from his lip from where I'd managed to hit him.

I glared at him, struggling against Nate's iron grip. "What? Are you going to beat me up again?"

Morgan didn't answer. He was busy searching for something on his phone.

"Get off of me!" I yelled at Nate, realizing I wouldn't be able to get enough leverage to force him off of me—he was too heavy. Still, I tried to kick and hit him as best as I could, though he was managing to restrain me well enough that it didn't make much of a difference.

"Ah, here it is," Morgan said, crouching down beside me. He held out his phone for me to see the screen. My breath hitched. I stopped struggling when I saw what it was he was so eager to show me: a picture of Jordan and me kissing in the parking lot outside the arcade.

"Don't," I pleaded, already knowing what he planned to do.

"Don't what?" He grinned menacingly.

I closed my eyes, willing myself not to cry, wishing I was anywhere else.

"You can't deny it anymore, fag. Soon the whole school is going to know what you are."

"Please don't," I pleaded, unable to stop a single tear from rolling out.

"Guys, maybe we shouldn't," Cole said from his position by the door. He wasn't looking at me, or either one of his friends. His eyes were trained on the bathroom sinks instead.

"You one of them now, Cole?" Morgan glared at him. "Are you a faggot lover?"

"That's not what I'm saying," Cole protested, finally looking at me. He couldn't stare for long, though, before having to look away again.

Morgan didn't seem convinced. I watched as he stood, taking slow steps toward his dark-haired accomplice. "Prove it," he said, shoving his cell phone into Cole's hands. Cole looked confused, so Morgan clarified: "Send it to everyone you know at this school."

"Why?" he asked, staring down at the phone. I could see something like conflict in his eyes—looking in that moment like he wished he was literally anywhere else.

"Because I said so," Morgan said, watching Cole's every move like a hawk.

Cole glanced from the phone to Morgan, then briefly to me before returning to the phone.

"Are you a fag, Cole?"

Something flashed in his eyes then, and for a moment, I thought Cole seemed afraid. "Fine," he said quickly. "I'll do it."

I watched as he typed on Morgan's phone, feeling my face grow paler by the second.

"I just sent it to myself," he told Morgan, handing back the phone. "I'll make a mass text tonight."

"You better," Morgan said, stuffing the phone in his pocket again. He turned to Nate. "Take his clothes off."

"What?" My eyes widened at Morgan's command.

Nate hesitated. He looked at Cole, who shook his head at him. Cole had a stern look on his face and seemed to be trying to communicate with Nate without actually opening his mouth.

"Fine, I'll do it myself," Morgan grumbled, reaching for my shirt.

"Get the fuck off me!" I fought against him, but still he managed to get my shirt over my head.

"Morgan, this is assault," Cole voiced as strongly as he could.

"Relax. I'm just making sure he doesn't leave this bathroom anytime soon," Morgan explained, tossing my shirt into the nearest toilet. "He can't be in the hallways without a shirt on, so he'll have to wait until everybody's gone for the day."

Neither Nate nor Cole responded.

Morgan looked down at me with a smirk. "Everyone will know you and lover boy's secret by tomorrow, Goldman, and there's nothing you can do to stop it."

More tears pooled in my eyes, but I did my best to blink them away.

"I pity you," I managed to say, looking up at my tormentor with as much bravery as I could muster. "For whatever hell your life must be if doing this to other people is the only thing that makes you feel like you're not completely worthless."

Morgan's face remained expressionless. He held my gaze for a few long moments before turning away. "Let's go," he said to the others. There was bitterness in his voice, and he walked past Nate and Cole without looking at either of them. Nate left next, but Cole lingered for a few moments more.

He slipped his phone into his back pocket before he whispered a faint, "I'm sorry," and walked out, following the others. Once alone, I slumped down, curled my knees to my chest, and sobbed into them.

I don't know how long I stayed there, or if anyone else came and went, but the next thing I was consciously aware of was a warm hand softly caressing my cheek. I looked up and blinked away my tears, seeing a gentle face staring back at me. I crawled forward and snuggled into Jordan's chest. He simply held me in his lap, gently rocking me as he weaved his fingers through my hair.

"I'm so sorry," he whispered.

SIC 'EM

"They've got a picture. They're going to out us," I choked out, twisting my fingers into the fabric of Jordan's shirt so he wouldn't disappear. I was terrified. Terrified of what would happen when everyone found out about me—about us—and terrified that he might leave me here.

I knew I wouldn't be able to face it alone this time. I cried harder. I didn't want to lose him.

Jordan hugged me tighter, doing his best to calm me down. "It's okay. It'll all be okay."

I tried to focus on his voice. I tried to let the whole world melt away, but all I could think about was the giant hammer that was about to fall down and crush us both.

I noticed then that Jordan had wedged a wooden door stopper under the closed door. It wouldn't keep someone out if they really wanted to get in, but it was enough to deter anyone who tried for now, and I was grateful for the small sense of security it gave me, because in this state, I definitely didn't want anyone to see me.

"I'm not ready," I whispered in a shaky voice.

"I'll be right here the whole time. I promise," he assured me, rubbing his hand up and down my back. It was soothing. I closed my eyes and let myself relax into him.

Ø

I must have fallen asleep in Jordan's arms, because the next thing I knew, I was being placed on a soft surface. A bed. My bed. Jordan then crawled in beside me and pulled me closer to him, and I took the opportunity to snuggle into his chest again.

He smelled good. He always did.

Once we were comfortable, he tucked my head under his chin and held me close. He draped his arm over my waist, and I felt somehow safer because of it. I was just about to fall asleep again when I heard his phone ring.

He cursed quietly and pulled it out of his pocket to answer. "Holly?" he asked softly, though I could feel his voice rumbling in his chest as he spoke. I was close enough to the phone to be able to hear her side of the conversation as well.

"Is Eli with you?" she asked.

"Yeah," Jordan said. "He's sleeping."

"Is he okay? I just saw what happened."

"Saw?" Jordan asked, sounding worried.

"There was a mass text. A picture."

"What kind of picture?"

"It's a pretty clear shot of the two of you kissing. You're outside of an arcade or something," she said. "They're asking people to share it."

"I'm going to kill them," Jordan hissed.

"You have to ask Eli first," she warned. "This is his fight, and as much as I hate him for it, he does tend to say no."

With my eyes closed and my face still buried in Jordan's chest, I reached up and took the phone from him. He seemed surprised that I was awake, but I didn't really care. I pressed the phone to my ear. "Holly?" I said, my voice still thick from exhaustion and tears.

"Yeah?" she asked, briefly pausing when she registered it was me.

"Sic 'em." I didn't wait for her response—I ended the call and dropped Jordan's phone somewhere on the bed. I vaguely heard him pick it up and place it on the nightstand, but I was more focused on other thoughts.

Holly would destroy them. She had been gathering shit on them for years, stuff even I didn't know, in anticipation of this moment or a moment like this—when I'd had enough of their shit and decided to push the big red button. They'd crossed a line with this one. Actually, they'd crossed a lot of lines, and now Holly was going to make them regret it.

"You okay, Elliot?" Jordan asked softly.

"I will be," I mumbled, pulling away just long enough to look up at his face. He was gazing down at me. My eyes wandered down to his lips and I slowly sat up. "Jordan?"

"Hm?" He was still lying down but looked up at me with mild curiosity.

"What was it like when you came out?"

"At school or with my family?" he asked.

"Both, I guess," I said, lowering my head to his chest and draping my arm over his stomach.

"Well . . . it was scary as all hell," he started, sounding uncomfortable as he dove into what I could only assume were painful memories. "I wasn't ready to come out to the school, but some of the guys on my soccer team walked in on me kissing one of the freshmen in the locker room. It was . . . humiliating. When they told the coach that I was gay and that they didn't feel comfortable changing in the same room as me, he made me go and change in the girls' locker room. It didn't last long, though, because eventually they taunted me to the point where I actually quit the team. There weren't many people who wanted to talk to me after that. I was kicked out of my normal lunch table and ended up finding refuge at the freshman unpopular table."

"That sounds horrible." I sympathized with him.

"It wasn't all bad." I felt him shrug. "I realized that I didn't want to be friends with people who were like that anyway, and I was actually happy with those freshmen for a while."

"What do you mean 'for a while'?"

"I was friends with this kid named Carson," he explained. "He was the target of a lot of bullying at school and had been even before I had met him. Part of it was because he was a pretty skinny, nerdy kid with a huge birthmark on his forehead, but most of it came from the fact that he was openly gay. He was a really nice kid, but eventually the bullying got to be too much. His parents and the police got involved after a particularly ugly incident and it ended in him moving away. I ended up losing my best friend, and I just wish I would've done more to help him before it got to that point."

"I'm sorry," I breathed.

"It's not your fault," he said, and leaned back against the headboard. "Come here."

I snuggled close to him and directed the conversation in a slightly different direction. "What about with your family then?"

"Well, I avoided telling them for a long time. My dad was kind of conservative, so I wasn't sure how he would react. I ended up telling my mom first, and she accepted me with open arms. But when my dad found out, it was . . . bad. He got violent, mostly throwing things. He cornered my mom one night and told her to choose between me and him, and, well . . . he left."

"Jordan . . ." I leaned on my elbows, hovering over him so that I could see his face. "I'm so sorry."

"Don't be. It's over now."

Looking down at him then, knowing how strong he'd had to be, I leaned down and pressed my lips to his. He was amazing, and I couldn't feel any luckier to have him.

I pulled away and smiled at him. "I like you, Jordan," I said honestly. "I like you a lot."

A small smile graced his lips. "I like you a lot, too."

KITTEN

Every snicker and whisper that reached my ears as I walked down the hallway at school that next morning was another nail in my coffin. It was better when I couldn't make out what was being said, as each muttered syllable lingered in my mind, slowly chipping away at my sanity.

No wonder he doesn't have any friends.

I knew it from the start.

I can't believe he's gay.

My only solace came from the warm fingers interlaced with my own. I squeezed Jordan's hand tighter as my chest became heavy. Breathing was all the more laborious and I felt the beginnings of an anxiety attack taking hold. In a moment of pure panic, I veered left and dragged Jordan down the hall to the nurse's office. We slipped through the door and I collapsed into the nearest plastic chair, burying my shaky fingers in my hair. "I can't do this."

Jordan didn't waste a second and knelt down in front of me, resting his hands on my knees. He looked me in the eye. "You're doing fine, Eli. Look—I'm right here, and I'm not going anywhere, okay? I don't care what any of them say. You're still the same strong, courageous, and undeniably adorable boy I fell in love with."

Love? He's in love with me?

All I could do in that moment was stare at him, my mouth partially open in anticipation of words that wouldn't come. My eyes started to water as I stared into his.

Jordan offered up a sly smile. "Don't go crying on me now, Eli."

I blinked away the moisture in my eyes. "I wasn't going to cry," I said stubbornly. "And I'm not adorable either."

"Elliot." He gave me a knowing look. "You are the most adorable thing I've ever laid eyes on."

I scowled and looked away, noticing then that there was no one else in the nurse's office. Lisa must have been off wandering in a different part of the school, or perhaps she hadn't even arrived yet. Either way, I was grateful for our moment of privacy. "I find that hard to believe."

Jordan appeared to drink in my features with so much adoration it almost made me melt. "That's because you don't see what I see."

"And what do you see?" I asked, eyeing him cautiously.

Jordan smiled and traced my cheekbone with his knuckles. "I see the mane of a lion: soft, golden, and untamed. I see its courage, but I also see that inside, that lion has the ferocity of a kitten. I see honey-brown eyes that look like liquid gold when they catch the sunlight at the right angle. But most importantly, I see you."

I couldn't think of a single word to say in response. I

had no idea he'd spent that much time thinking about me.

"Look, Eli. I know this isn't the best of times, but I know how I feel, and I know that I never want to let you go. I want to be able to hold you and kiss you and call you mine whenever I'm able. I want to protect you and help you and love you for as long as I can. I want to be your boyfriend, officially, and I want you to be mine. What do you say?"

I sat there frozen, taking in his hopeful expression. His words echoed in my mind, and I realized I was struggling to remember how to breathe.

"I—" I took a deep breath. "I don't know how anyone could refuse you after that."

Jordan chuckled and squeezed my hands. "Is that a yes?"

A small smile tugged at the edges of my lips. "Yes."

A wide grin immediately spread across Jordan's face. He jumped up and enveloped me in a tight hug. "I'm so happy!" he practically squealed in my ear, lifting me slightly and spinning us around.

"As happy as when I told you I was gay?" I asked, smirking.

"Even more so." He set me back down and planted another small kiss on my forehead. He grabbed my hand. "Now come on, kitten. We need to get to class before the bell rings."

"Oh no," I warned as he dragged me out into the hallway again. "You are not calling me that."

"Calling you what?" he said innocently, though he knew exactly what I meant. I narrowed my eyes at him, but he just chuckled. "I have no idea what you're talking about."

Huffing in frustration, I let him drag me all the way to our lockers, and then to my first-period classroom. It was only after he let go of my hand and told me he'd be back after class to walk me to my next one that I realized something important: Jordan had just stopped me from having a panic attack. He'd distracted me so well that I'd completely forgotten about the critical eyes and whispers that had caused it in the first place. In fact, I barely noticed any of that as he dragged me through the hallways.

I had a boyfriend now, and that made me so happy that I did not care one bit about the awkward stares and whispers that followed me as I made my way to my seat. I had Jordan, and right then, that was all I needed.

THE BIG RED BUTTON

I was feeling a bit uneasy as we made our way into the cafeteria. In fact, I wanted nothing more than to turn around and run for the hills. But the weight of Jordan's hand in mine anchored me to reality.

It was so much worse here than it was in the hallways. In the halls, people were forced to spread out, with only a few eyes to follow us at a time. But here . . . it was all of them. There were so many people, and I felt like they were all looking straight at us. My chest tightened—it felt as if the walls were closing in around me.

Then Jordan made the whole world freeze with just a few simple words:

"You okay, kitten?"

"We really need to sit down and have a serious discussion about that nickname," I muttered.

"You don't have to pretend to hate it, Eli. I can see it in your eyes. You absolutely love it when I call you kitten."

"I do not," I protested under my breath. I could feel

heat rising to my face, painting my cheeks a light shade of pink.

"What was that, kitten?" Jordan teased me, his smile brightening all the more when I glared at him. I rolled my eyes, and then looked down and was startled to see that we were already at our table. He had distracted me again.

God, he was perfect.

I sat down beside him and across the table from Holly. I stared at her, noting the smug grin on her face as she typed away at her laptop. "Holly?"

"Last chance to pull back the reins," she said without making eye contact—her eyes were glued excitedly to her screen.

I felt Jordan's hand resting on my knee. I looked at him and he gave me an encouraging smile in return. I had no idea what to expect from her, but whatever it was, I was ready.

I turned back to Holly and nodded. "Do it."

Her smile widened at that. "Good, because I already pulled the trigger earlier this morning." She finally looked away from her laptop and leaned forward, whispering conspiratorially: "Stage one: humiliation." With that, she tapped a button on her keyboard and steepled her hands together, training her eyes on a group of girls in the far corner of the cafeteria. I was confused at first, but then everything started to make sense.

I watched with piqued interest as one of the girls, Stella—Morgan's girlfriend, point of fact—rose from her seat after a few seconds with a murderous look on her face. Her eyes remained glued to her phone screen as she grabbed a milk carton with her perfectly manicured fingers and stomped over to her boyfriend, seated at another table.

"You lying bastard!" she screeched, pouring the milk into his lap. He leaped up in surprise, staring down at his soaked crotch before turning his rage to the short brunet. It was at that exact moment that Holly pulled out her cell phone and sent a text.

"What the fuck, Stella?" Morgan said, arms spread wide, expecting an explanation. All eyes were glued to the unfolding scene. "What was that for?"

Stella responded with a swift slap to his face. "You *cheated* on me?" She sounded simultaneously hurt and furious. "With *Gracie*?"

"What? No, I didn't!" he exclaimed, desperate to save his own skin, but even I could tell from the high pitch in his voice that he was lying through his teeth.

"Then what's this?" she asked, showing him her phone.

His face grew visibly pale. "Where did you get that?" he demanded.

She opened her mouth to answer but was cut off when a fuming Nate entered the cafeteria.

"We need to talk," he growled as he approached Morgan, ignoring Stella completely.

"I'm kind of in the middle of something," Morgan said in an irritated tone.

"I just got kicked off of the goddamn football team," Nate hissed back. "Someone tipped Coach off to where I keep my stash." His voice lowered in volume as he approached the end of the sentence, probably because he realized he had an audience, but it was still audible from where we were sitting.

"He had drugs?" I asked Holly in a whisper.

"Weed mostly," she confirmed under her breath, enthralled by the scene playing out before her eyes.

"Don't look at me." Morgan raised his hands. "I didn't snitch."

"Then who the fuck did?" Nate asked, fuming.

"I don't fucking know!" Morgan's voice was even higher due to his rising state of incredulity.

"Well, as far as I know, you and I were the only—"

He was cut off when the doors to the cafeteria swung open, revealing a tall, dark-haired, drop-dead handsome boy who I was quite certain did not go to this school.

"Jason?" Cole stood up from his seat, eyes wide. He immediately backed away from the rapidly approaching boy. He wasn't fast enough, though, because the boy— whose name was apparently Jason—reached out, grabbed Cole's shirt, and slammed their lips together.

"Holy shit!" I looked at Holly in surprise. "Cole is gay?"

"It seems as though he's been using you as a target to keep them off of his own scent," she said, smirking.

"What are you—" Cole stuttered as Jason pulled away.

"You've turned into a real asshole since you left, Cole." Jason let go of him with a look of disgust. "Popularity suits you well. I hope it was worth it." Then Jason turned on his heels and exited the cafeteria, leaving Cole with a panicked expression. All eyes were now upon him.

When Cole couldn't take it anymore, he ducked his

head and made for the nearest exit, leaving his two fuming friends in the cafeteria to fend for themselves.

"We're over, Morgan," Stella said with her nose in the air. She turned and started back toward her seat. She didn't make it very far, though, before Morgan stopped her with another question.

"Who sent you that picture?" he asked, furious.

"Holiday Tucker." She sniffed and stepped well away from him.

Holly waved innocently as Morgan's eyes snapped to her, not even bothering to deny the fact that she was the culprit. I noticed she had a bit of a twinkle in her eye, and realized then that she was thoroughly enjoying herself.

The boys were finding out firsthand what happened when you messed with someone whom Holiday Tucker cared about. And it wasn't over yet.

"Stage two: regurgitation," Holly muttered as Morgan stomped across the cafeteria. Nate followed closely behind his humiliated friend, having no doubt figured out that his dismissal from the team was also due to the red-haired she-devil sitting in front of me. I felt my anxiety build with each step closer they took.

Seeing how quickly and significantly the situation was escalating, Jordan stood up and positioned himself in such a way that he could, if necessary, jump in front of either me or Holly. I stood up too—mostly so I could get myself out of the way if things turned sour, though I wasn't about to admit that out loud.

"You're dead meat, Tucker," Morgan growled when he was close enough to cause harm.

"Ah, ah, ah." Holly waved her finger condescendingly, grinning ever wider. "I'm not finished yet."

I knew from experience that Morgan didn't like being talked to like that. I had a feeling that this whole thing was going to end with someone inside of a body bag.

"What?" Morgan practically spat, stopping when he reached our table, which, thankfully, served as a barrier between him and Holly.

"We-l-l," Holly rose from her spot, meeting his glare with one of her own, "when somebody threatens my friends, I take it upon myself to find out why. Obviously, Eli did nothing to you, so the source of the bullying must have originated internally. So I did a little research." She glanced at her laptop and tapped a few keys. She looked at the boys, turning her piercing gaze to Nate. "Let's take a look at you, shall we? Born in eastern Michigan and given up by your mother immediately after your birth, you bounced around foster homes for your entire life. You were adopted by the Anderson family two years ago and are now one of six children. It seems as though you are simply craving attention."

"No, I'm not," he denied, stepping forward.

"Or perhaps it's that you want someone to feel just as alone and helpless as you've always been. Or as dejected as you felt when Ellie Goldman rejected you."

"I don't have to listen to this shit!" he shouted before turning and stomping away.

Next up, Holly turned to Morgan. She glanced at her screen again. "And you're merely trying to escape the hell created by your alcoholic father."

"You'd be wise to keep your mouth shut," Morgan threatened.

"You have no control in your own home. You feel helpless against the wrath of your father, so you do everything you can to regain that control and make others feel helpless while you're here."

"Shut up! Shut up! Shut the fuck up!" He surged forward then, attempting to climb over the table—to grab Holly or hit her, I didn't know and was thankful not to have to find out. Jordan stepped in front of him at the last second, to keep him from doing any damage, but before anything could happen the intercom came on, stopping Morgan in place: *"Morgan Cook, Nathan Anderson, and Cole Decker, please report to my office immediately,"* the principal announced. Though he'd tried to sound neutral, a clipped impatience seeped through his words.

Morgan froze where he stood. He scowled at Holly. "This isn't over," he said in a threatening tone.

"No, it's not," Holly agreed as she watched him walk away. When he was out of earshot, she added, "There's one more stage."

"What's the last stage?" I asked.

With a smirk, Holly sat down and turned her computer to me. "Incrimination." On the screen was a grainy cell phone video of Morgan and Nate attacking me in the bathroom the other day. I watched as Morgan stripped me and threw my shirt into the toilet.

"How did you get that?" I asked in a small voice, unable to look away even though I wanted to.

"Cole recorded it," she revealed. "And then he sent it

to me. He told me to use it to help you, and that he deserved whatever punishment came his way."

I sat back and blinked. Cole had tried to stand up for me a couple of times—he'd attempted to get Morgan and Nate to stop whenever they took things too far, but I realized then that he was too scared of them to really say no to either one of them. If he made one wrong move, their aggression could have easily turned his way.

"I sent the video to the principal," Holly said, closing her laptop. "I also threatened to call the police if he refused to do anything about it."

"I don't want to get the police involved," I said, shaking my head.

"They have been continuously harassing and attacking you for years, Eli. This school chooses to believe that bullying is not a problem. They would rather turn a blind eye than actually sit down and deal with this issue. This is one of the only ways I could think of to make sure they can't ignore it any longer. It's not just harassment anymore. What they are doing is a hate crime now. It's a serious offense. At least this way the school will be forced to do something about it. They'll probably suspend them, maybe even expel them, and if they don't, the police will deal with those three accordingly. If it all goes according to plan, you'll finally be free from them."

It sounded too good to be true. Could it really end just like that? I looked up at Jordan, unsure, and then at Holly. "Thank you," I said softly.

She nodded, offering an understanding smile. "That's what friends are for, Elliot."

Just then, the intercom came on a second time. The

office receptionist's voice came through the speaker: "*Jordan Hughes and Elliot Goldman, please report to the front office.*"

Right then, I felt Jordan's hand slip into mine. I took a deep breath and prepared myself to answer a lot of uncomfortable questions. But then Jordan lightly squeezed my hand, and whatever happened, I knew it would all turn out just fine in the end.

AFTERMATH

By the time Jordan and I got to the main office, Morgan was just finishing up with the principal. Nate and Cole still sat in the row of chairs directly outside of his door, waiting for their turn. Nate sat in the rightmost chair and had his head leaning back against the wall as he stared at the ceiling tiles. Cole was bouncing his knee up and down anxiously while he stared at the blank wall in front of him. He sat in the middle of five chairs, leaving a one chair gap between himself and Nate. Unfortunately, that meant that one of us would have to sit next to Cole, and upon seeing this, Jordan did not hesitate to sit in the closest seat to him. Tension grew in Cole's posture as he shifted away from Jordan a bit, and I figured that was probably because he already had proof that Jordan had no qualms about punching him in the face. I took the leftmost seat in the row, right next to Jordan, and the farthest possible from Nate, and did my best to relax.

Moments after I sat down, Morgan exited the principal's

office, looking like a pissed bull ready to charge. I subconsciously leaned closer to my boyfriend, seeking any form of comfort he could give me as I watched the boy fume past us. The principal emerged seconds later to call Nate into his office, and as soon as the boy had disappeared inside, Cole got up and moved down a seat. We all relaxed a little at the increase in distance, but we were still by no means comfortable. I was just glad Jordan was there, or I might have suffocated in all the tension.

The sound of the ticking clock on the far wall became almost maddening. It was only interrupted by the occasional typing on a keyboard or shuffling of papers from the receptionist's desk. When her phone rang suddenly, I jumped a little in my seat.

"You okay?" Jordan asked in a low tone, no doubt noticing how on edge I was.

I tried to distract myself by reading the various announcements and promotional posters displayed around the main office, but it was hard. I didn't really care about volleyball sign ups or five tips for staying organized, so my mind was quick to wander to other things.

Like what on earth was going through Cole's mind right now. He'd just been outed, too, and unlike me, he didn't have a Jordan to support him. Sure, he had been an asshole to me for the last couple of years, and finding out that he was gay didn't change that or mean that he was forgiven, but we had something in common now. I couldn't help but feel a little sympathy. We were going through the same thing at the same time, just from opposite sides, both trapped.

Nate came out of the office then, his face completely pale. He looked afraid, probably because he had never been caught doing anything bad before. I was at least glad to see that he knew there were consequences for his actions now. He didn't make eye contact, and instead moved past us like a spirit wandering through a completely different plane.

Cole stood and followed the principal into his office when the man looked at him. He had his head bowed and closed the door gently behind him.

Seeing that there were no longer any immediate threats, Jordan loosened up and turned to look at me. "Are you doing okay?"

"Yeah," I breathed. "Peachy."

He studied my face for a moment, trying to figure out what I was really feeling. I'm sure it wasn't hard for him to recognize my anxiety. My nerves were in a palpable fog surrounding my body right now, and it was undoubtedly showing in some form or another.

"Good." Jordan relented, grabbing my hand and interlacing our fingers. "Because everything is going to be okay."

I exhaled slowly, focusing on the warmth of his hand in mine. How did he always know what I needed to hear?

We sat in silence then, patiently waiting.

When Cole finally came out again, he looked surprisingly relieved. His face and posture were calm, accepting, and as he passed us, he even offered a small smile. I watched as he walked up to the receptionist and quietly asked her, "Can you call my aunt to come pick me up?"

When I looked back, I saw the principal stepping out

of his office. He looked at both Jordan and me, then down at our joined hands, and let out a tired sigh. "Come in, you two."

Knowing Jordan would be in there with me made me feel immediately better. I didn't want to answer questions alone. It was embarrassing and awkward trying to explain to an adult that you were being bullied.

Jordan helped me up from my seat and didn't let go of my hand as we followed the principal into his office.

"Thank you for coming here, boys," he said. "Please, take a seat."

I nodded, gulping nervously as I sat in one of the small chairs in front of the principal's desk. Jordan sat in the other.

"I assume you both know why I've called you in here?" he said, sighing. We nodded. "I've been informed about a bullying problem in this school and would like to hear your sides of the story. Please, tell me what's been going on."

Jordan looked at me, which I guess was my cue to go first. "The three of them have been picking on me for a long time," I started.

"How long?" the principal asked, leaning forward on his elbows as he listened to what I had to say.

"Since middle school." I shrugged. "It started off as just verbal stuff, but eventually it got more physical."

"In what way?" he asked.

"There's the stuff that you see in the video, and there've been a few other instances where they've beaten me up worse," I said.

"I see." The principal glanced at his computer screen.

"I'm sorry," Jordan interjected, "but I have to add to that. What they've been doing is more than just roughing him up. Last month I found him after one of these instances. They left him lying on the ground at the back of the school. He was covered from head to toe in bruises; he had blood running down his face, a broken nose, and could barely stand up on his own."

"Why didn't you say anything about this?" the principal asked, looking back to me.

I shrugged weakly. "Nobody asked."

"The violence and harassment also increased when they suspected Elliot was gay. That's getting into hate crime territory," Jordan said, reiterating what Holiday had said only a short time earlier.

"I assure you, Mr. Hughes, it is being addressed now," he said.

"Good," Jordan said, and quieted down a bit.

The principal turned back to me. "I have a system in place for dealing with situations regarding bullying, but as you know, these situations aren't always so black and white. You were the victim, Mr. Goldman. I want to know what you feel is justice for their behavior before I decide on what actions to take."

I didn't want that much pressure riding on me, so I just shrugged. "I don't know," I said. "But I will say that they were each bullying me to different degrees, so they shouldn't all have the same level of punishment. Morgan and Nate got physical and definitely acted with some degree of homophobia. Cole never laid a hand on me. Most of the bullying from him was verbal, and he even tried to stand up for me a few times and get them to stop when the other two were taking it too far."

The principal nodded. "How do you feel about expulsion?" he asked.

"I know that if Morgan or Nate were to come back to school, the bullying would likely continue, and with even more aggression. Expulsion is probably best for them. I think Cole has learned his lesson, though. If the other two are gone, he won't feel pressured into bullying others anymore. I hope."

"So, you feel as though a suspension is the best course of action for him?" the principal asked.

I nodded. "Yes."

"Okay." He wrote a few things down on a notepad he had on his desk. "I will take that into account when I dole out their punishments. Is there anything else either of you would like to add?"

"When you call my parents," I said, "could you leave out the parts about me being gay?"

"It's not our policy to out our students," the principal said. "All right, you two may return to your lunch period. I sent the boys home after our chat, so you won't have to worry about them for the rest of the day. I will be calling all the parents tonight to notify them of this incident and of the consequences."

"Thank you, sir," I said, standing up alongside Jordan. We made our way to the door.

"Oh, and Elliot?" I turned. "Please notify us sooner the next time something like this happens."

"Yes, sir," I said, ducking my head as I exited his office.

Once we were back out in the hallway again, Jordan slipped his hand into mine. "How are you doing?" he asked softly.

"I'm surprisingly okay," I said, relieved that I wouldn't have to deal with the bullying anymore. It was almost serene in a way. I felt like I was in a dream.

"Good," Jordan said, squeezing my hand reassuringly. "I'm glad."

I smiled at him, knowing for the first time that everything was going to be okay.

Ø

Everything was surprisingly peaceful after Morgan and Nate were expelled, and Cole was suspended. And to be honest, it was really nice being able to hold Jordan's hand in public. My parents were concerned about the extent of the bullying after they received the call from the principal, and upset that I hadn't told them about it sooner, but we worked it out, and I felt less alone for the first time in ages.

More of the kids at school than I realized seemed to actually be okay with us being gay. Some even showed and voiced their support. If anyone had any problems with us, they now kept it to themselves.

It seemed as though Morgan and Nate were the catalysts for all the hate I had been receiving, and in the aftermath of their expulsion, it all just kind of fizzled out into a quiet, general acceptance.

"Hey," Jordan said as we stopped at my locker so I could grab a textbook for my next class.

"Yeah?"

"How do you feel about prom?" he asked, his head tilted slightly.

"Prom? I don't know, why?"

"I was wondering if you'd maybe like to go with me," he said nervously. "If you wanted to go at all, that is."

"I don't know . . . dancing?" I said with uncertainty. "I'm pretty sure I have two left feet."

"I could show you all of my killer dance moves," he offered.

I raised a single skeptical eyebrow. "Is that killer as in good, or killer as in anyone who is subjected to watching you may suddenly and unexpectedly drop dead from having witnessed a crime?"

"No comment," he chuckled. "Come on, Eli. It could be fun."

"Fine." I relented. "As long as you're there it can't be that bad."

"Awesome," he said, grabbing my hand again as I closed my locker door. "I can't wait."

"Me neither," I agreed, and squeezed his hand contentedly. I had never really planned on going to prom, but with Jordan, I was ready for anything.

BIRTHDAY PARTY

"You can do this, Eli," I said, giving myself a pep talk as I checked myself out in the mirror. It was my eighteenth birthday. And Ellie's. She was no doubt downstairs, socializing with all our relatives who assumed when we said that dinner was starting at six, we really meant for them to start showing up at three.

I had been down there earlier for a little while, but upon seeing that it was approaching five thirty, I disappeared to my bedroom to calm my nerves a little and make myself look more presentable. Today was the first time Jordan was coming to my house as my boyfriend. I hadn't told my parents we were dating. Not yet at least. But the thought of him being so close and keeping my relationship with him a secret was a bit nerve-racking. I'd had a conversation with him about it already, and he respected my decision that I wasn't ready to come out to my family yet. Hopefully, that meant everything would go smoothly tonight, but I was still a bit paranoid.

I smoothed my hair in the mirror for what must have been the hundredth time, all while doing my best not to freak out. I pulled out my phone and checked for any messages from him. There weren't any new ones, just one from twenty minutes ago that said he was trying to find something and that he was almost ready. When I saw the time, I started to panic a little internally.

He was going to be here any minute now.

"All right, birthday boy," Ellie said, scaring the crap out of me as she poked her head into my room. "You're beautiful. Now come downstairs and socialize."

"Don't call me beautiful," I huffed. I looked over at her. She had lightly curled her long blond hair and was actually wearing a dress for the first time in what felt like forever. It was white with a blue-and-green-themed floral pattern all over it. "You look nice today."

"Thank you," she said, accepting my compliment while looking down at her outfit. She looked up again and informed me, "Nana just got here. You better come down and see her before she starts hunting you down."

I laughed. "Okay. I'll be down in a second."

She nodded before disappearing, heading back downstairs. I turned and scanned myself in the mirror one more time, attempting to smooth down my hair before following my sister.

At the bottom of the stairs a body plowed into me and nearly knocked me over, squeezing me like an anaconda trapping its prey. All the breath left my body in one giant wheeze.

"Nana," I choked out. "Nana, I . . . can't . . . breathe."

"And I can't find my dentures. We all have problems." Thankfully, she released me and proceeded to ruffle my hair.

Sigh. So much for that.

"They're in your mouth, Nana," Ellie commented as she walked by.

"Right again, little Einstein," she called after my sister. Then she turned back to me and grabbed my chin, turning it side to side as she assessed my features. Satisfied, she released me and beamed. "Happy eighteenth birthday, nugget!"

"Thanks, Nana." I internally prayed that she would refrain from using that nickname when Jordan showed up.

As if I'd summoned him, there was a knock at the door. I used the distraction to my advantage and excused myself, escaping the scrutiny of my bat-shit crazy grandmother.

I threw open the door, expecting to find Jordan there but instead found Holly holding two boxes in her hands.

"Happy birthday, Eli," she greeted me, startling me as she pulled me in for a hug.

"Thanks," I said, awkwardly patting her leather jacket-clad back. It was odd for Holiday to show affection in ways as gentle as hugging. More often she showed it through teasing and revenge plots, so I wasn't exactly sure how to respond. Thankfully, she pulled back before I really had to.

"Heads-up," she said without much warning and tossed me one of the boxes in her hands. I fumbled as I tried to catch it. It bounced off my hands a couple of times, but I somehow managed to snag it before it hit the floor.

I straightened back up, the box now in hand, and looked back at Holly; however, she had taken the opportunity to slip past me and was already calling for my sister.

"Eleanor!" she shouted at the top of her lungs.

"What?" Ellie shouted back just as loudly, popping her head around the corner.

Holly grinned at her friend. "You're an adult now. Do you know what that means?"

"Uh . . . I can register to vote?" Ellie said, uncertain about which answer Holiday was looking for.

"No, it means you're even more boring than you were before," Holly teased.

Ellie rolled her eyes. "If I'm so boring, then why do you hang out with me?"

"Because I'm exciting, so you balance me out."

Ellie shook her head. "Whatever. Come on, I need to go raid the snack table again."

Holly lit up a little more. "Did you get dill pickles?"

"Yep. Just for you," Ellie said, leading the way to the kitchen.

I smiled. It was nice to see my sister relaxing and being playful again. I had been beginning to think she was a robot programmed to do nothing but study.

Realizing I was still standing in the open doorway, I reached for the door to close it again. It was then that I caught sight of Jordan's car pulling over to park on the side of the street in front of my house, since the driveway was already full. I suddenly found myself caught in that awkward position where I didn't know if I should close the door and wait until he came up and knocked or stand there with it open, watching him like some overexcited creep while he got out of his car and walked all the way over to me.

In the end, I set Holly's gift down on the small table by

the door where everyone kept their keys and then stepped outside, closing the door behind me.

"Hey," I breathed as he approached, rubbing my arms to fight the December chill. There were big fluffy flakes of snow falling from the sky, and though he'd only been outside for a few moments, they were already collecting on his hair like a halo.

"Happy birthday, kitten." He wrapped me in a warm hug. I nuzzled my face into his chest as I wrapped my arms around him. If I could've purred in that moment, I probably would have, which only helped to solidify his nickname for me. He always smelled so good.

"Thank you," I said as we pulled apart. Glancing at the door again, a pinprick of panic overtook me once more. "Just a reminder: my family is crazy, and for your own benefit, I advise you to socialize as little as you possibly can with my grandmother."

"It'll be fine, Eli." He chuckled slightly and ruffled my hair.

I huffed in frustration. "Okay, fine. Let's go in," I muttered while running my fingers through my hair again in a pathetic attempt to tame it.

I opened the front door and we stepped inside. I figured most of the family would be gathered in the kitchen by now, where my mother was undoubtedly trying to pass my casseroles or pies off as her own creations by throwing them in the oven at the last second.

"Mom," I called as I rounded the corner, stopping midthought when I saw her in the middle of committing an atrocity. "Don't you dare add oregano," I said, warning her.

Frowning, she slowly withdrew her hand and capped the container, placing it back in the spice cupboard. Satisfied, I gestured behind me. "Everyone, this is Jordan. He's one of my friends from school."

"Nice to meet you, hon—" my aunt Deborah started to say, but was cut off by Nana.

"Boy, I'd take him with a side of milk and cookies."

"Nana!" I said, my face turning pink with embarrassment.

"What?" she asked as if I was the odd one. "He's a hot tamale!"

"You're not so bad yourself." Jordan winked flirtatiously at my grandmother. I gave him a look, silently pleading with him not to encourage her.

"Oh, I like this one," Nana said with a smirk.

"Okay," I said, inserting myself into the conversation. "That's enough of that. We're going to go upstairs."

Ellie and Holly exchanged a look. My mother, wonderfully oblivious, only replied with, "Okay, honey. Food will be ready in about an hour."

"Okay," I acknowledged before leading Jordan up to my room. I only knew I needed to get him away from my family.

And that I really wanted to kiss him.

MY GIFT TO YOU

As soon as Jordan had cleared the doorway to my room, I closed the door and locked it. Upon hearing the faint click, he turned around and smirked. "Expecting something, kitten?"

"No," I said, blushing, looking down at my socks. Jordan stepped forward and lifted my chin with a single finger.

"Are you sure?" he asked, tilting his head slightly. He leaned forward a little.

I let out a ragged breath, my eyes dropping to his lips. He took another step forward, trapping me against the door. He slid his fingers under the hem of my shirt and traced them along the bare skin above my hips, sending goose bumps all up and down my body. Leaning all the way forward, he pressed his lips to the base of my jaw and let them travel down my neck at a tortuously slow pace.

He sucked on my earlobe, and I closed my eyes and let out a low, rumbling moan. He released a short laugh in response. "You even purr like a kitten," he mused.

M. MONTGOMERY

"Shut up," I hissed playfully, as he chuckled and returned to kissing my neck.

"You know," he whispered into my ear, "it *is* your birthday."

"And?"

"And I still have to give you your present." I felt him smirking again.

"Oh," was all I could say.

Jordan pulled back to look at me. He grinned mischievously as he wrapped his arms around my lower waist and hoisted me into the air. I squealed briefly before he dropped me on my bed, causing me to bounce. My breath hitched as he hovered over me, his arms on either side of my torso and his nose mere inches from my own.

He stayed there for a few moments, taking in my flushed features. Just when I was starting to wonder why he was waiting so long, he chuckled.

"Get your mind out of the gutter, kitten," he said as he reached into his pocket and pulled out a small wrapped box, which he placed on my chest. "Happy birthday."

I propped myself up on my elbows while Jordan shifted into a seated position. I grabbed the box from my chest before it could fall and sat up. I stared at him with a glint of curiosity but received only a contented grin in return. Returning to the box, I carefully pulled off the ribbon and unwrapped it, and, stealing another curious glance at Jordan, removed the lid.

I don't know what I was expecting, but it wasn't what I found inside. I tipped the box on its side and caught in my other hand a small stone figurine that rolled out. I held it up to get a closer look.

"It's a little lion for my little lion," Jordan said. He placed his chin on my shoulder and wrapped his arms around my stomach. "My gift to you."

"Jordan," I began, but lost my words as I moved my fingers over the smooth surface of the figurine. On the stomach of the lion, I found two letters carved into the stone: E and J.

"It's to help with your kitten courage," he explained while softly nuzzling my neck. "Do you like it?"

I turned to face him, grinning, and pressed my lips to his. I somehow managed to set the lion off to the side before I wrapped my arms around his neck and forced him to lay down with me on top of him. I pulled away from him, laughing, and stared into his mesmerizing eyes. "I love it."

"I love you," Jordan replied without hesitation, looking at me with pure adoration. It made my heart flutter. A stupid grin tugged at my lips. Staring at him, I realized just how amazing this boy really was and how he made me feel all giddy and warm inside with the simplest of gestures. A blush crept up to my cheeks. I dropped my head into the crook of his neck and started to explore it the same way he had explored mine earlier.

He wriggled beneath me with each brush of my lips. He gripped my hips tightly as I licked, sucked, and tugged at his skin. His squirming made me painfully aware of his ever-growing problem. Pride bloomed in my chest at the notion that I had caused his flustered state.

"Careful, Elliot," he groaned. His voice was hoarse and he tightened his hold on me.

I worked my way back up to his ear, whispering, "I love you too."

It took all of two seconds for him to get over his initial shock at what I'd said, and he flipped us over. He didn't waste a second as he attacked my mouth with a hungry, passionate kiss.

"I love you, I love you, I love you," he murmured, each time almost pulling away from my lips. It made my heart swell. As his tongue plunged into my mouth and his hand found its way into my hair again, a shiver traveled down my spine, causing my back to arch upward. I pressed into him, and my toes curled. Then I slipped my fingers under his shirt and traced his abs. He groaned at my touch. When he couldn't take it anymore, he ripped himself away and quickly pulled his shirt up over his head, flinging it to the side.

When did he start straddling me?

I made an inhuman sound as he rolled his hips. He matched it with one of his own. "Fuck, Jordan," I croaked, my breath coming out in uneven spurts, my body moving on its own as if to match his motions.

"If you insist." He tugged my shirt over my head and started to unbutton my pants. In that moment, my body was screaming with desire while my mind was screaming in panic.

"Wait," I said through heavy panting. I grabbed his wrists to stop him. His eyes latched onto mine, waiting for my next words. "I'm not—I don't think I'm ready for . . . *that* yet."

Jordan leaned over me until our faces were aligned

once more. He looked down at me with a small smile and asked, "Then what *are* you ready for, Eli?"

I wanted to say something, but at a slight shift between our bodies, I closed my eyes and rode out a small wave of pleasure. I wasn't sure then what my mind wanted, but I knew what my body needed.

When I opened my eyes again, I was staring up at Jordan. The words left my tongue before I could think to stop them.

"I'll drip if you swirl."

EPILOGUE

"Why did I agree to this?" I asked, tugging at my collar. Everything about the suit I was wearing made me uncomfortable. The fact that I was surrounded by a bunch of my classmates outside of regular school hours was totally outside my comfort zone, making things even worse.

"I don't know, but you look really cute in that tux," Jordan said, smiling.

"Well, the lighting is dim," I reasoned, looking out at the horde of hormonal teenagers dancing under colorful lights. This year's prom theme appeared to be Hollywood and film related. I had to admit, the decorations weren't bad. There was even a red carpet running down the middle of the venue.

"Why do you always deflect my compliments?" he asked, pouting.

I smiled flirtatiously as I grabbed the front of his jacket and pulled him closer. Pushing myself onto the tips of my toes, I leaned in and muttered in his ear, "Because it's the only thing that prevents me from turning into a pile of mush."

"Do you want me to stop then?" he teased, pulling back a little to show me a raised eyebrow. He made sure to put his hands on my waist to keep me from going too far, though.

"Never," I smiled, placing a quick kiss on his cheek.

"You two are really cute together." It wasn't a new voice, but it was an unexpected one. I turned to see Cole Decker and that guy, Jason, who'd kissed him in the cafeteria. They came over to us.

"Thanks," I said. "So are you."

Cole rubbed the back of his neck as a light blush tinged his cheeks. He looked at his partner for a moment before his gray eyes settled on me again. "Look, Eli," he began, "I wanted to say that I'm sorry. For everything."

"It's okay," I told him. I had forgiven him already, he just didn't know that yet.

"But it's not okay," he said, fidgeting with the buttons on his jacket. "I was bullied when I was forced to come out at my last school. I know how much it sucks. I had some other pretty traumatic stuff hit me at around the same time the bullying started, so by the time I moved here, I was so paranoid about it happening again that I made some pretty stupid decisions to try to avoid it. I'm sorry."

"I forgive you," I said, smiling reassuringly. "Just promise me something, okay?"

"Anything," he said, eager to hear what I was about to say.

"From now on, I want you to be who you are, and I want you to be proud of it."

"I think I can manage that." Cole nodded and turned to the other boy. "Come on, Jason. Let's go see what they've got for snacks here." Jason's piercing blue eyes lit up at the mention of food, and he happily let Cole drag him through the crowd.

As I watched them go, my mind replayed the conversation we'd just had. Was I proud of who I was? Completely?

"What are you thinking about?" Jordan asked. He must've seen the puzzled look on my face.

I looked up at him, doubt flooding through me at an idea that kept recurring in my mind. "I think I want to come out to my parents," I blurted. I couldn't keep it to myself anymore. As long as I was keeping this part of myself a secret, I couldn't truly be proud of who I was.

"Really?" he said, a little surprised by my statement.

"Yeah," I said with a little more confidence.

"When?"

"Tonight." More definitive this time.

"Okay." A proud smile appeared on Jordan's face. "Do you want me to be there or not?"

I thought about it for a moment, biting my lip as some of the confidence started to wear away. What if they didn't accept me? I nodded. "Yeah, I want you to be there."

"Okay," he said again. "I will be."

"Do you think they'll accept me?" I asked nervously.

"I think everything is going to turn out just fine," he assured me.

I looked down at my shoes. "Hey," he said, pulling my attention back to his face. "Do you want to dance?"

"I'd love to," I said, and wrapped my arms around his

neck just as a slow song started to play. In that moment, I knew that whatever happened tonight, I would still have Jordan.

Ø

"You picked a great night to introduce me as your boyfriend," Jordan commented as we ascended the front steps to my house. I looked over to see him glancing down at his tuxedo, smoothing it out a little. "I'm already all dressed up."

I laughed, grateful to him for lightening the mood a little. "Very true," I said, smiling as I opened the front door. I walked inside and found my parents in the living room. Dad was watching some documentary on the TV while Mom was reading a book.

"Hi, honey. Hi, Jordan," she greeted us, looking up and smiling. "How was the dance?"

"Good," I breathed, looking at Jordan for a brief moment of reassurance before I continued. "There's actually something kind of important that I wanted to talk to you about."

Hearing the nervousness in my tone, my father paused his documentary, and my mother closed her book and sat up straight.

"What is it, sweetheart?" she asked curiously.

"Well," I bit my lip, unsure of how to phrase it. Glancing back at Jordan, I decided to just go for it. "Jordan is my boyfriend."

They didn't say anything at first. Dad stared at Mom

and they seemed to be having some sort of nonverbal communication. After a moment of the two of them just staring at each other, my mother looked over and asked, "So you're gay?"

"Yes," I said, unsure if this was going well or not.

My dad swore under his breath then and I felt my stomach sink. He suddenly got up out of his recliner and left the room. I was starting to panic, but was confused when he returned shortly after that with his wallet in his hands. He unfolded it, pulled out a twenty-dollar bill, and handed it to my smug-looking mother.

"You two bet on my sexuality?" I asked incredulously. Jordan started to crack up beside me. I turned and glared daggers at him as well. "I can't believe you guys," I huffed.

"We got bored," my dad said, trying to defend himself.

I shook my head. "So that means you guys are cool with it?" I asked, unimpressed by their behavior.

"Of course, Eli," my mother said. "We love you no matter what."

"Yeah," Dad tacked on. "Just keep it PG while I'm in the house."

"Dad," I said, feeling my cheeks going red.

Jordan chuckled again. "Well, I should be getting home," he told me. "It's getting late."

"Okay. See you tomorrow?" I asked hopefully.

"Of course." He smiled and kissed me on the cheek. "Love you."

"Love you too," I said. In fact, I don't think I'd ever felt more loved than I did in that moment.

I even loved myself.

ACKNOWLEDGMENTS

For being the catalyst of my writing journey, my first thanks goes to my friend Stevie. She not only introduced me to the wonderful world of creative writing but also became my first reader, my first editor, and my first co-author. Every story I have ever written exists because of her, and for that, I am eternally grateful.

Next, I would like to thank Melody Kruger, who, in addition to teaching me how to use proper grammar, told me that she could hear my voice in my writing at a time when I didn't believe I had a voice at all. Though I only had her as a teacher for a short time, she had a big impact on who I am today. She taught me that everyone makes mistakes, and that it's what we learn from them that really matters.

I would also like to thank Monica Pacheco, Andrew Wilmont, Deanna McFadden, Rebecca Mills, and everyone else on the Wattpad team who helped me get my book ready for publication. Without them, *Lab Partners* likely would have never reached its full potential.

My family deserves a huge thank you as well for being supportive during the publication process despite the fact that I gave them little to no information about what was actually happening. I love you guys.

Lastly, I owe the biggest of thanks to Chris, Becca, Cammi, and Angela, who were forced to endure my endless complaints about my unhealthy stress levels throughout this whole process. The fact that none of them ran away is frankly astounding to me, and even though I know they didn't understand half of the things I ranted about, I was just happy that they let me vent.

ABOUT THE AUTHOR

Raised in a small Michigan town, Mora Montgomery learned early on that she was a bit of an outcast. Instead of trying to blend in with her peers, she embraced what made her different, and dove headfirst into the things she loved. Persistence in her studies earned her a college degree a month before she graduated from high school, and a dedication to music allowed her the freedom to play multiple instruments and use them to fund her way through college. This motivation will enable Montgomery to graduate with two engineering related degrees by 2023. *Lab Partners* is her first published work.

Wrestling team captains Max Desera and Axel Cortés must settle their long-standing rivalry - but a different kind of fire may ignite between them.

FIGHTING FIRE WITH FIRE

EDEN YOUNG

Read the Free Preview
on Wattpad

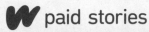

Check out the latest titles from Wattpad Books!

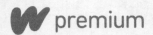

wattpad

Where stories live.

Discover millions of stories created by diverse writers from around the globe.

Download the app or visit
www.wattpad.com today.

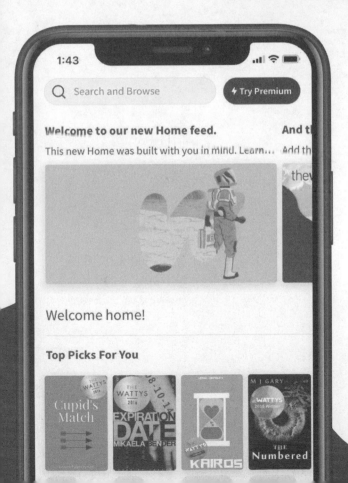